REMEMBER THE FEAR

(A Clara Pike FBI Thriller —Book 1)

Molly Black

Molly Black

Bestselling author Molly Black is author of the MAYA GRAY FBI suspense thriller series, comprising eleven books; of the RYLIE WOLF FBI suspense thriller series, comprising six books; of the TAYLOR SAGE FBI suspense thriller series, comprising eight books; of the KATIE WINTER FBI suspense thriller series, comprising eleven books (and counting); of the RUBY HUNTER FBI suspense thriller series, comprising five books (and counting); of the CAITLIN DARE FBI suspense thriller series, comprising six books (and counting); of the REESE LINK mystery series, comprising six books (and counting); of the CLAIRE KING FBI suspense thriller series, comprising seven books (and counting); of the PIPER WOODS mystery series, comprising eight books (and counting); of the GRACE FORD mystery series, comprising eight books (and counting); of the CASEY BOLT mystery series, comprising seven books (and counting); of the JADE SAVAGE mystery series, comprising seven books (and counting); of the ELISE CLOSE psychological thriller series, comprising five books (and counting); of the TESSA FLINT mystery series, comprising seven books (and counting); and of the CLARA PIKE FBI suspense thriller series, comprising five books (and counting).

An avid reader and lifelong fan of the mystery and thriller genres, Molly loves to hear from you, so please feel free to visit www.mollyblackauthor.com to learn more and stay in touch.

ISBN: 979-8-89482-564-9

BOOKS BY MOLLY BLACK

ELISE CLOSE SUSPENSE THRILLER
BEHIND HER LIES (Book #1)
BEHIND HER SMILE (Book #2)
BEHIND HER SECRETS (Book #3)
BEHIND HER GATES (Book #4)
BEHIND LOCKED DOORS (Book #5)

CLARA PIKE FBI SUSPENSE THRILLER
REMEMBER THE FEAR (Book #1)
REMEMBER THE DEAD (Book #2)
REMEMBER THE LIES (Book #3)
REMEMBER THE SILENCE (Book #4)
REMEMBER THE PAST (Book #5)

TESSA FLINT MYSTERY SERIES
BARELY SEEN (Book #1)
BARELY HEARD (Book #2)
BARELY FORGOTTEN (Book #3)
BARELY MISSING (Book #4)
BARELY ALIVE (Book #5)
BARELY THERE (Book #6)
BARELY SILENT (Book #7)

JADE SAVAGE MYSTERY SERIES
ALL SHE FEARS (Book #1)
ALL SHE WANTS (Book #2)
ALL SHE REMEMBERS (Book #3)
ALL SHE NEEDS (Book #4)
ALL SHE HIDES (Book #5)
ALL SHE DREADS(Book #6)
ALL SHE LOST (Book #7)

CASEY BOLT MYSTERY SERIES
BROKEN (Book #1)

FLAWED (Book #2)
BLEMISHED (Book #3)
DAMAGED (Book #4)
TWISTED (Book #5)
FRACTURED (Book #6)
TAINTED (Book #7)

GRACE FORD MYSTERY SERIES
NEARLY MINE (Book #1)
NEARLY SAFE (Book #2)
NEARLY FREE (Book #3)
NEARLY GONE (Book #4)
NEARLY HIS (Book #5)
NEARLY LOST (Book #6)
NEARLY DONE (Book #7)
NEARLY NEXT (Book #8)

CLAIRE KING MYSTERY SERIES
ONCE HE SEES (Book #1)
ONCE HE LONGS (Book #2)
ONCE HE TAKES (Book #3)
ONCE HE FEELS (Book #4)
ONCE HE KNOWS (Book #5)

MAYA GRAY MYSTERY SERIES
GIRL ONE: MURDER (Book #1)
GIRL TWO: TAKEN (Book #2)
GIRL THREE: TRAPPED (Book #3)
GIRL FOUR: LURED (Book #4)
GIRL FIVE: BOUND (Book #5)
GIRL SIX: FORSAKEN (Book #6)
GIRL SEVEN: CRAVED (Book #7)
GIRL EIGHT: HUNTED (Book #8)
GIRL NINE: GONE (Book #9)
GIRL TEN: WANTED (Book #10)
GIRL ELEVEN: VANISHED (Book #11)

RYLIE WOLF FBI SUSPENSE THRILLER
FOUND YOU (Book #1)
CAUGHT YOU (Book #2)
SEE YOU (Book #3)

WANT YOU (Book #4)
TAKE YOU (Book #5)
DARE YOU (Book #6)

TAYLOR SAGE FBI SUSPENSE THRILLER
DON'T LOOK (Book #1)
DON'T BREATHE (Book #2)
DON'T RUN (Book #3)
DON'T FLINCH (Book #4)
DON'T REMEMBER (Book #5)
DON'T TELL (Book #6)

KATIE WINTER FBI SUSPENSE THRILLER
SAVE ME (Book #1)
REACH ME (Book #2)
HIDE ME (Book #3)
BELIEVE ME (Book #4)
HELP ME (Book #5)
FORGET ME (Book #6)
HOLD ME (Book #7)
PROTECT ME (Book #8)
REMEMBER ME (Book #9)
CATCH ME (Book #10)
WATCH ME (Book #11)

RUBY HUNTER FBI SUSPENSE THRILLER
IF I RUN (Book #1)
IF I TELL (Book #2)
IF I LIVE (Book #3)
IF I FORGET (Book #4)
IF I RETURN (Book #5)

CAITLIN DARE FBI SUSPENSE THRILLER
COME GET ME (Book #1)
COME FIND ME (Book #2)
COME TAKE ME (Book #3)
COME CATCH ME (Book #4)
COME SAVE ME (Book #5)

REESE LINK MYSTERY
BEYOND REASON (Book #1)

BEYOND REACH (Book #2)
BEYOND REPAIR (Book #3)
BEYOND DOUBT (Book #4)
BEYOND NORMAL (Book #5)

PIPER WOODS FBI SUSPENSE THRILLER
SOMEWHERE SAFE (Book #1)
SOMEWHERE SANE(Book #2)
SOMEWHERE WHOLE (Book #3)
SOMEWHERE FAR (Book #4)
SOMEWHERE WRONG (Book #5)
SOMEWHERE HIDDEN (Book #6)
SOMEWHERE DARK (Book #7)
SOMEWHERE SILENT (Book #8)

PROLOGUE

Jessica Hanley's boots clicked methodically against the cobblestones, the only sound breaking the stillness of the night. Moonlight draped over her shoulders like a shawl, casting her vibrant red hair in a halo of silver threads. She walked alone through the promenade, an old place where shadows clung to the edges like dark secrets.

The night was beautiful—a canvas of obsidian sky punctuated with stars that shimmered like distant lighthouses. The air was crisp, carrying the scent of dew-laden grass and blooming night flowers, their perfume lingering long after she passed them by. Ancient trees lined the path, their leaves whispering softly. Everything about this place should have offered comfort, should have been soothing—an oasis of tranquility in the chaos of life.

Yet, Jessica was consumed with a profound sadness, so tangible it seemed to seep from her very pores and blend with the midnight air. Her eyes, usually bright with creative fervor, now mirrored the sorrow that weighed on her soul. In the quiet of the night, her heart throbbed painfully, each beat a reminder of the emptiness within.

Her steps slowed, her breaths deepening as she tried to savor the peacefulness around her, to let it seep in through her skin and fill the void. But peace was a language her spirit seemed to have forgotten how to speak, its vocabulary replaced by a lexicon of loss and yearning.

She moved like a specter among the delicate lacework of light and shadow, her presence an intrusion upon the serene landscape. With every step, she felt as though she were sinking deeper into a sea of grief, waves of memories threatening to pull her under.

Jessica continued her solitary walk, her figure a contrast against the perfection of the night. The world around her slumbered peacefully, unaware of the storm raging inside her—a tempest of emotions with no eye, no calm center to offer respite. As the stars above blinked down at her in silent commiseration, she could not escape the heaviness that darkened her path, nor the ominous sense that something more than heartache waited for her in the shadows ahead.

Jessica's heart pulsed against the stillness, a metronome ticking off seconds that stretched into eternity. Her feet carried her unbidden toward the silhouette of an old oak tree, its branches a tangled canopy against the starlit sky. She paused beneath it, recalling how its leaves had once whispered secrets to a young woman with dreams in her eyes.

The bark was rough under her fingertips, the same texture it had been all those years ago when she and Michael had carved their initials within a heart—a cliché act of youthful romance now overgrown by time and indifference. Michael. The mere thought of him sent a ripple through her chest, as if her heart recognized a name it hadn't dared utter in ages.

This was where he had ended things, right under this ancient oak. She remembered the confusion, the disbelief, how the setting sun had painted his face in hues of gold and red, as if mocking her with its beauty while her world crumbled.

"Jess, I'm sorry," he had said.

She had come expecting a proposal, and instead, with those three words, he became the one who got away.

She traced the outline of their initials, the carving partially healed by time's relentless passage, much like her own heart—scarred but never fully recovered. In her mind's eye, she saw Michael walking away from her for the last time, his figure growing smaller until it blurred into nothingness. That image had haunted her, becoming the yardstick against which every subsequent relationship was measured and found wanting.

He had moved on, of course. She'd heard about his life through the grapevine of mutual acquaintances—an accidental eavesdrop here, a social media snippet there. A new love, a burgeoning family, a happiness that seemed so distant from her own reality. All the while, Jessica remained tethered to this spot, to the ghost of a first love that refused to be exorcised.

As the night wrapped around her, the air held a chill that seeped into her bones, making her shiver—not from the cold, but from the realization that some part of her had never left this place. It lingered here, eternally waiting for a different outcome, for the words that would rewrite history. But no matter how many times she willed things to be different, the ending remained the same.

Jessica's steps quickened as she sought to outrun the sorrow nipping at her heels. She felt the quiver of her chin, the telltale sign that the dam within her was about to break. Her hands clenched into fists at her sides, nails digging into her palms in a futile attempt to anchor herself to the present. She could not succumb to the weakness, not here, not now. And yet, as the memories flooded back, they brought with them a tide of tears that blurred the tranquil path ahead.

Jessica stumbled forward, her breath catching in her throat. A sob clawed its way out, shattering the silence of the night. It echoed off the trees, a lone testament to her heartache—a sound so raw, so profound, it seemed to startle the very air around her. She pressed on, each step heavier than the last, her face glistening with the sorrow she could no longer contain.

The promenade lay deserted, a winding ribbon of cobblestones that led to nowhere and everywhere all at once. Benches dotted the pathway, and Jessica found herself drawn to one of them, its wrought-iron frame cold and unyielding beneath her trembling fingers.

With a weary sigh, she sank onto the bench, her gaze drifting across the water that shimmered like glass under the light of the stars. She drew in deep, shuddering breaths, attempting to stitch the fabric of her composure back together. The night seemed to hold its breath with her, the stillness punctuated only by the distant call of a night bird—a somber lullaby for her fractured soul.

Her mind replayed the scene over and over—the finality of Michael's words, the closing of a chapter she'd never wanted to end. Here, in this spot, she'd been left with a scar that time refused to heal. As she sat, the tears finally began to abate, leaving behind the hollow emptiness of loss. She looked up at the sky, the constellations tracing patterns of forgotten legends and tales of love lost to the ages.

Jessica felt the solitude envelop her, a cloak woven from strands of melancholy and resignation. This bench, this place, held too much of her—fragments of laughter and whispers, now ghosts in the cool night air. It was a purgatory of her own making, where hope and despair danced a ceaseless waltz.

Yet, in the shadows that lingered just beyond the reach of the lamplight, there was an ominous sense of something more. It prickled at the edges of her awareness, a whisper of danger that teased the periphery of her senses. Jessica wrapped her arms around herself, seeking comfort in the cocoon of her own embrace, unaware of how closely fate was watching, ready to unfold its dark wings upon her solitary vigil.

Her breath formed transient clouds in the chill air, each one dissipating as quickly as it appeared, a mirror to her fleeting attempts at composure. The park was a tableau of darkness pierced by sporadic pools of lamplight, casting elongated shadows that stretched across the footpath like fingers reaching out from the night. It was in this interplay of light and shadow that Jessica caught a movement, subtle yet distinct—a shifting silhouette that seemed both part of the darkness and separate from it.

Her heart skipped a beat, patterning out an erratic rhythm that matched the quickening cadence of her thoughts. She told herself it was just someone out for a late stroll, perhaps another soul seeking solace under the mantle of midnight. As the figure drew closer, however, its presence felt imposing, a weight in the atmosphere that pressed down on her with an almost tangible force.

"Evening," she murmured, her voice barely rising above a tremulous whisper, expecting some sign of acknowledgment—a nod, a greeting, anything to cut through the tension that gripped her.

But the figure remained silent, its approach measured and deliberate. Jessica squinted into the dark, trying to discern features, intentions, humanity within the approaching form. Then, as it stepped into the fringe of lamplight, a glint of metal caught her eye, stealing her breath with its cold promise.

A knife.

It hovered in the air, an extension of the shadowy figure's hand, reflecting a sliver of light that seemed to mock the serenity of the night. Panic surged through Jessica's veins, hot and urgent, as she realized the true nature of this encounter. This was no benign passerby come to offer comfort or concern; this was threat made flesh, a harbinger of malice poised at the precipice of violence.

She knew she should scream, run, fight—anything to resist the fate that now loomed before her. But fear had rendered her mute, her body frozen in disbelief even as her mind screamed for action. There was a surreal quality to the moment, as if time itself had slowed to allow her to note every detail—the way the blade seemed to dance with a life of its own, the almost imperceptible shift of weight as the figure prepared to strike.

Jessica's eyes locked onto the gleaming edge of the weapon, a razor-thin line between life and death, and in that sliver of steel, she saw her future reflected back at her—fractured and fading fast.

CHAPTER ONE

Clara sat rigid at the breakfast table, the mahogany surface gleaming under the early morning sun that filtered through the bay window. The fine china before her was arrayed with meticulous care, a silent testament to the routines that had governed her childhood home for as long as she could remember. Her mother's flair for perfection was evident in the crisp linen napkins folded into swans, the silverware aligned with geometric precision. Yet today, the usual chatter of shared anecdotes and light-hearted jests was replaced by a thick silence that seemed to press against the walls of the dining room.

Her father, a man usually punctuated by a robust laugh and an insistence on hearty breakfasts, sat slumped, his eyes darting from the untouched eggs Benedict to the ornate clock on the mantelpiece as if time itself were an accomplice to the tension that hung over them. Clara herself felt a knot tighten in her stomach, not from hunger, but from a palpable sense of foreboding that seemed to emanate from her parents like a distress signal she couldn't quite decode.

She shifted her gaze across the room, noting the way the dust motes danced in the shafts of sunlight, casting patterns on the polished oak floor. The scent of freshly ground coffee lingered in the air, mingling with the faint aroma of bacon that now lay cold and congealing on their plates. Despite the unease that gripped her, Clara couldn't help but catalog every detail—the way the morning light played off the crystal decanter of orange juice, the delicate sound of the grandfather clock ticking in the hallway, the slight creak of her mother's chair as she adjusted her posture ever so slightly.

Each sensory impression etched itself into Clara's memory with unnerving clarity—her mind, a vault that collected and preserved moments with obsessive care. It was a trait that served her well in her profession, where the smallest observation could unravel a case or unveil a truth long buried. But here, in the house where she had grown up, it was a curse. Every sight, every smell, every imperceptible shift in the atmosphere was a reminder that something was profoundly amiss.

The muted drone of the television seeped into the room like a sinister fog, unnoticed by Clara's parents, who sat across from her, their expressions hollow. Their gazes were fixed somewhere beyond the floral-patterned curtains, lost in silent contemplation or perhaps resignation. Yet, Clara's eyes flickered toward the screen where breaking news crawled along the bottom edge, each word imprinting itself indelibly in her mind.

"Local authorities are continuing the search for nine-year-old Jake Pike, who was last seen..." The reporter's voice was steady, but it carried an undercurrent of urgency that belied the practiced neutrality. Clara's sharp eyes absorbed the photograph of the boy displayed on the screen—an image burned into her psyche, his wide-eyed innocence juxtaposed with the grim reality of his disappearance.

Her mother's hand trembled slightly as she lifted her coffee cup, the liquid untouched and cooled, while her father stared at his plate, the eggs now congealed and unappealing. Neither reacted to the grim parade of facts spilling from the television. But Clara, she listened; she couldn't help but listen.

Then, the shrill ring of the phone shattered the morose tableau. A chill ran down Clara's spine, her nerves firing a warning as though the sound was not merely a call but a harbinger. The ringtone, piercing and insistent, felt like it was slicing through the layers of silence that had settled over the house since her brother's disappearance.

Her mother flinched, a small jerk of the head, as if waking from a trance. Her father's hand paused midair, the fork he held hovering above the untasted breakfast.

Clara's breath caught in her throat, a premonition tightening its grip around her chest. The ringing continued, each tone echoing through the room, bouncing off the walls, filling the space with its ominous melody. Even without picking up, Clara knew what would follow—the officer telling them they'd found a body. Her mother collapsing in a heap. She'd lived the moment once in this house and a thousand times in her mind's eye.

***

Clara's heart jolted as the sharp trill of a ringing phone tore through the silence of her subconscious, dragging her from the tangled depths of a nightmare. Her eyes snapped open, her gaze darting around the room, still haunted by the lingering shadows of her dream. The digital clock on her bedside table glowed a stark 6:07 AM against the backdrop of darkness, its steady pulse an anchor in the disorienting transition between worlds.

The ring persisted, insistent, shattering the early morning's calm and setting her nerves on edge. With a trembling hand, she reached out, fumbling for the source of the intrusion. Her fingers grazed the cool surface of her cell phone, and she drew it closer, squinting against the bright screen that cut through the gloom like a beacon.

"Mom," the caller ID announced in bold, impersonal letters. Clara's breath hitched, her mind reeling as she registered the name that had become a ghost in her life. They hadn't spoken in more than a year, not since the chasm of grief and unspoken accusations had wedged itself between them. The shock of seeing that name now sent a tremor through her body, the tendrils of dread from her nightmare bleeding into reality.

She rolled over, the weight of her mother's name pressing down on her like a physical force. The room seemed to contract around her, the familiar contours and shadows taking on a sinister quality in the half-light. Her photographic memory played cruel tricks on her, summoning up images of their last encounter, each detail etched with vivid, painful clarity—the strain in her mother's eyes, the set of her father's jaw, the way the air had grown thick with things left unsaid.

Clara wrestled with the impulse to let the call go unanswered, to wrap herself back in the cocoon of sleep and forgetfulness. But the ringing was relentless, a siren song that spoke of urgency or desperation. With a resigned sigh, her training as an FBI agent nudging her toward duty, she swiped at the screen, her voice barely above a whisper as she braced for the onslaught of emotions that would surely follow.

"Hello?" Her voice sounded foreign in the stillness, a crack in the veneer of solitude that had become her refuge. The silence on the other end of the line was heavy, charged with words yet to be spoken, with history yet to be reconciled. And in that moment, suspended between the remnants of her nightmare and the unknown implications of this unexpected call, Clara felt the keen edge of vulnerability, the sense that the world she knew was about to shift beneath her feet once more.

"Mom?" Clara's voice was a careful blend of surprise and wariness, the syllables falling into the silence that seemed to fill her apartment like smoke.

"Clara," came the reply, the word wrapped in the familiar timbre of maternal warmth, yet hollowed out by the chasm of time and distance between them. "I hope I didn't wake you."

The conversation stumbled forward with the cautious dance of estranged relatives, each probing the boundaries of the other's life without crossing into intimacy. They spoke of weather patterns and trivial news items, the mundane chitchat serving as a buffer against the weight of unspoken truths. Clara listened, her mind cataloging every hesitation in her mother's voice, every shift in cadence. Her FBI training had honed her ear for subtleties that others might miss, but today it was her daughter's intuition that picked up on the tremor of anxiety beneath her mother's practiced nonchalance.

"Mom, is everything okay? How's Dad doing?" Clara ventured at last, steering the conversation toward the heart of her unease.

The pause that followed was brief, but to Clara's acute senses, it screamed volumes. When her mother spoke again, her words were coated with a resignation that seemed to seep through the phone line.

"Your father… We're not… together anymore, Clara," her mother confessed, each word deliberate, as if she were navigating a minefield of emotion. "It's been almost a year. We're getting divorced."

The air in Clara's lungs felt suddenly thick, and she fought to keep her composure. Her parents' marriage, once the bedrock of her childhood, had crumbled away without her even knowing it. She could almost see the courtroom in her mind—a stark, sterile place where lives were dissected into legal documents and assets divided with surgical precision. The fact that her family had fractured so completely, and yet so silently, from her own world left her feeling disoriented, as if the ground was slipping away beneath her feet.

"Divorce," Clara echoed hollowly, the word resonating with the sterile finality of a case file being closed. Her mother's voice continued, explaining details about lawyers and proceedings, but Clara's trained memory had already begun to wander, sifting through past interactions for missed clues, analyzing conversations verbatim for hidden fractures. That her mother chose now to tell her, when legalities demanded disclosure, stung with a particular sharpness. It was an afterthought, a footnote in the narrative of her family's dissolution.

"Thanks for letting me know," Clara managed, her tone measured, betraying none of the turmoil that churned within her. Her thumb hovered over the "End Call" button, a digital guillotine waiting to sever the tenuous thread of her family connection. The air in her apartment seemed to grow heavier, pressing down on her shoulders like an unseen burden as she finally let her thumb fall, cutting off the final empty words from her mother. With the line dead, Clara sat motionless, the phone still clutched in her hand, her heart hammering against her ribs in betrayal. Her gaze drifted across the room, each familiar object blurring into a tableau of normalcy that felt like a veneer over the raw wound her mother's news had inflicted.

The silence was oppressive, amplifying the dull throb of hurt that pulsed through her. But before Clara could sift through the flotsam of emotions, the ringtone pierced the quiet, a shrill siren that dragged her back to reality. She glanced at the caller ID, her trained instincts kicking in despite the emotional turmoil. It was the Bureau. Work. Duty. A lifeline thrown to her sinking form. She wiped away the single tear that had escaped her control and steeled herself for what was to come.

"Agent Pike," she answered, her voice steady, belying the chaos that reigned just moments before.

"There's been a murder," said the terse voice on the other end of the phone. "We'd like your eyes on it."

"Understood. I'm on my way," Clara replied. Her response was automatic, her mind already shifting gears, compartmentalizing her personal anguish to make room for the professional detachment necessary for the task ahead.

She rose from her seat, her movements precise and deliberate. She slipped into her jacket, grabbing her badge and gun, the familiar weight of them grounding her. As she crossed the threshold of her apartment, she left behind the remnants of her previous life, stepping out into the cold clarity of her role as an FBI agent. The day awaited her, sinister and unknowable, hiding secrets only she could unearth.

CHAPTER TWO

Clara Pike's polished shoes clicked rhythmically against the gleaming floor of the FBI headquarters in Washington, DC, her sharp gaze sweeping over the familiar hive of activity. Agents bustled about with the weight of secrets and public safety on their shoulders, their faces etched with determination and the burden of knowledge. The air was thick with the scent of black coffee and worn leather, mingling with the faint hum of fluorescent lights overhead.

The building itself was a fortress of justice, its corridors lined with photographs of most wanted criminals, reminders of both victories and ongoing battles. Clara passed under the shadow of the proud FBI insignia, feeling the usual twinge in her stomach—a concoction of adrenaline and a relentless drive for answers.

"Clara," a voice called out, anchoring her back to the present.

Derek Morales stood by the elevators, his posture relaxed but eyes revealing a storm beneath the surface. He was the counterbalance to Clara's detail-oriented nature, a seasoned profiler who navigated the murky waters of criminal minds. His presence was a balm to the chaos that sometimes threatened to engulf her thoughts, his intuition guiding her when the details threatened to consume her.

"Got the file," Derek said, holding up a manila envelope. "Director Shaw signed off on it just now."

Clara approached, nodding her appreciation. She knew that within the confines of that folder lay a labyrinthine puzzle waiting to be solved, each piece a step closer to understanding the depravity they were about to face.

"Let's head out," Derek continued, gesturing toward the exit. "You can dig into the details while I drive."

They made their way through the maze of desks and white noise, each step bringing them closer to the reality of their grim task.

The brisk air greeted Clara as she stepped outside, the chill wrapping around her like an unwelcome shroud. The FBI headquarters loomed behind her, its stoic windows reflecting the steel gray sky. She followed Derek's purposeful stride across the pavement, his shoulders tense beneath the fabric of his coat—a testament to the weight of the case ahead.

The ride to the crime scene would be another descent into darkness, a path Clara had walked many times before. But for now, as she slid into the passenger seat of their unmarked vehicle, she focused on the feel of the file in her hands, the potential clarity it could bring to the chaos.

Derek started the engine, and the car merged into the flow of traffic, becoming one more anonymous player in the theater of the city. Clara opened the file, her eyes absorbing the opening words like a whisper from the abyss.

The file was thin—the details limited. Clara soaked them all in, determined to absorb even the most minute detail, but she knew from experience that nothing captured on those pages would compare to the reality of witnessing the crime scene in person.

"What makes this a federal case?" she asked, her tone edged with clinical curiosity. "We usually don't get called in for straightforward homicides."

"Ah," he replied, a note of gravity entering his voice as he navigated onto a quieter road. "This one's on federal land, which puts it squarely in our jurisdiction."

"Jurisdictional technicalities," Clara mused aloud, the words leaving her lips like smoke. She pondered the implications, her mind already racing ahead to construct the framework of possibilities. The fact that the murder occurred on federal land meant layers—layers of bureaucracy, certainly, but also potentially layers of meaning. What drew the killer there? Was the location chosen for convenience, or did it hold some deeper significance?

As the car swept around a bend, the dense canopy of trees lining the road seemed to press in closer, their branches casting skeletal shadows that danced across the hood of the car. Clara felt a familiar tightening in her chest, the anticipation of confronting the abyss once more.

"Hard to say anything until we get there," Derek began, his words slicing through the dense air of the car. "But based on the file, I'm thinking this was personal. Someone wanted to make her suffer—make a spectacle of it."

"I agree," Clara said. "Using a knife—slitting her throat, that's an up close and personal way to kill."

The sleek black SUV rolled to a stop, its tires crunching the gravel underfoot like a harbinger of the grim tableau awaiting them. Clara stepped out into the chill that had settled over the area, her breath forming fleeting clouds that dissipated in the air as quickly as they appeared. Her gaze swept across the scene—the police tape cordoning off the area, the uniformed officers maintaining the perimeter, and the forensic team huddled around something she couldn't yet see.

Clara's heart thrummed against her ribs, an involuntary response despite the years of training and countless crime scenes that had come before this one. The forest surrounding the clearing stood sentinel, its trees swaying solemnly with the whispers of a wind that carried the scent of pine and something darker—a metallic tinge that spoke of bloodshed.

She followed Derek, who navigated the uneven ground with a familiarity born of similar experiences. They approached the nucleus of activity, the starkness of the investigators' white suits a glaring contrast to the verdant backdrop. She pulled on her own gloves with methodical precision, preparing herself for the intrusion into a life violently halted.

As she walked, the gravity of her responsibility bore down upon her—it was not merely about solving a crime, but about restoring a narrative to the one who could no longer speak. She braced herself, knowing that every detail held a potential key, and with Derek at her side, the silent promise to uncover the truth pulsed between them like a current charged with shared determination.

CHAPTER THREE

"Remember, deep breaths," Derek murmured as they approached the scene, shooting her a sidelong glance that showed his understanding of the maelstrom of memories each new case stirred within her.

"Always," she replied, though her voice was barely audible above the cacophony of crows arguing in the treetops. Their calls seemed to mock the mortality below with raucous abandon.

The yellow crime scene tape fluttered in the wind, creating a discordant rhythm that seemed to echo the chaos of the night's events. Local PD, huddled together like dark silhouettes against the pale light of early morning, turned their attention to her and Derek as they approached.

"Agents Pike and Morales?" A stout officer with a furrowed brow stepped forward, his hand extended in greeting. His nameplate read "Sgt. Mitchell."

"That's us," Derek replied, shaking the sergeant's hand firmly.

"Thanks for getting here so quick," Sergeant Mitchell said, his voice carrying a weight of urgency. "We secured the scene best we could, but there's not much to go on."

Clara listened intently, her eyes scanning the perimeter. She noted the position of each patrol car, the distribution of officers, the layout of the nearby buildings—a row of converted warehouses with windows like blind eyes watching over the patch of ground where the body lay.

"Victim's name is Jessica Hanley, a local graphic designer," Mitchell continued, checking his notes. "Body was found by a jogger early this morning. No witnesses have come forward yet."

"Any signs of struggle?" Clara asked, her mind already racing with possibilities.

"None that we can see," he answered. "From the look of it, I think she probably went quick. Small mercies, I suppose."

Clara nodded, though she found it hard to think of anything connected to a murder investigation as an act of mercy.

"Thank you for containing the scene," Derek said. "We'd like to take a closer look, if you don't mind."

"Of course," Sargent Mitchell said, stepping aside and gesturing toward the location of the body.

The crime scene was meticulously cordoned off, the forensic team moving about with practiced precision. As Derek and Clara came closer, they were greeted by a figure in a white lab coat—Dr. Jenna Hargrove from forensics, whose eyes were weary but sharp behind the clear protective goggles.

"Agent Pike, Agent Morales," she greeted with a curt nod, flipping open her clipboard. "Preliminary findings are sparse, but the positioning of the body is… deliberate. Almost as if this was some sort of cleansing or healing ritual."

Clara took in Jenna's words, considering the significance. "Anything else you can tell us?"

"Time of death is estimated between midnight and two AM. He got the carotid, so the murder was precise and swift, but he cleaned all of the blood off of her…" Jenna hesitated, then leaned in closer. "I don't know. There's something about the whole thing that…the way he staged the body. She suffered a gruesome death, but it's almost like he tried to make her look—peaceful."

Derek frowned. "I didn't get that from the file, but you're right. Seeing it here now, there's definitely something about it that feels staged. Intentional. Like he's trying to send a message or complete some sort of mission."

"Thank you for sharing your insights, Jenna," Clara interjected. "We'll need to see everything you've got once you're done here. But for now, I think we need a closer look at the body."

"Of course," Jenna said, stepping back to let them pass.

As they moved forward, Clara felt a seed of recognition planting itself deep within her. The ominous feeling that gripped her was not just from the chill in the air or the grim tableau ahead. It was the sense of a pattern emerging, the outline of a killer's signature slowly coming into focus. And if this was a killer with a signature—with a pattern—then it was highly unlikely Jessica was his only victim.

The soles of Clara's boots crunched on the frost-covered grass as they approached the lifeless body, marking a stark contrast to the hushed whispers of the officers scattered around the scene.

Knowing what was coming, Clara steeled herself, feeling the psychological weight of her gift—or curse—settle upon her shoulders. A photographic memory like hers came with a price; every crime scene was a gallery of horrors she could never unsee. She couldn't just shake off a crime scene visit the way Derek could. Each image would live in her mind forever, often appearing unbidden in horrifying, vivid clarity. But it also made her an unparalleled asset in this grim theater of forensic artistry. Each detail she committed to memory was a potential clue, a silent witness to the transgressions enacted here under the cloak of darkness.

Her eyes touched upon the outline of the body, and she began her mental documentation. The positioning of the limbs spoke of careful placement, deliberate and precise. The hands were folded, almost as though in prayer or rest, and her eyes were closed—likely a choice the killer had made postmortem. She noted the pallor of the skin, an ashen gray against the vibrant green canvas of the park.

Clara moved closer, her gaze sweeping over the tableau. She circled the corpse, her senses attuned to every variance. The dew-laden blades of grass told tales of weight and movement; the displaced earth whispered of last steps taken. Clara absorbed it all, the images crystallizing in her mind's eye, locked away for later when they would be called upon to speak their truths. In her line of work, everything mattered—the fallen leaf, the angle of repose, the posing in the hands that Jenna had rightly observed as peculiar.

The early morning light filtered through the leaves, casting long, slender shadows that danced across the ground and over the body, accentuating the eerie stillness. Clara's eyes narrowed, scrutinizing the scene before her, dissecting each element with clinical precision. Her mind, a vast and organized archive of every case she had ever touched, began to whir with activity. Something nagged at her—a memory, elusive yet persistent, clamoring for attention amidst the silent screams of the scene. She had seen something like this somewhere before.

She stepped closer, leaning down to examine the angle at which the body rested. The clean line of the blade, the folding of the hands, it all held a haunting familiarity that resonated with a chilling echo in her mind. Clara's heart rate quickened as she recognized the similarity, as if the killer had left his signature with morbid artistry.

She closed her eyes, and an image filled them, clear and sharp as the day she'd first seen it earlier that week. It had just been a shadow in her periphery then—a picture on a murder board at a precinct she saw in passing. Still, she had seen it, and her brain had catalogued it, which meant she could pull it back up now, inspecting every detail.

The face in her mind's eye belonged to a young woman named Cassie Marlowe. A teacher, she had been found in her school's auditorium, her throat slit and her body displayed not unlike the figure before Clara now. The photographs she'd seen played across Clara's internal screen, vivid and unyielding. The same slit throat, the folded hands, the tilt of the head mimicking a grotesque mockery of repose.

Clara withdrew slightly, her breath a little shallower as she processed the visual overlap between the two crime scenes. Two women, both sharing an eerily similar fate, the choreography of their last moments mirroring one another in a sinister ballet.

A shiver crawled up Clara's spine as she pieced together the images in her mind, the implications forming a dark cloud over her thoughts. The coincidence was too great, the details too aligned. Whoever had taken these women's lives had done so with a message or mission in mind, communicated through the deliberate arrangement of their final pose.

The silence of the woods pressed in on her as she reluctantly tore her gaze away from Jessica's body, her mind racing with questions and the shadow of a dawning realization that this was only the beginning of a much darker puzzle.

"Hey." Derek's voice cut through her reverie, grounding her back to the present. "You okay? You look like you've seen a ghost."

Clara turned toward her partner, his familiar presence a steadying force amidst the turmoil of her thoughts. "Derek, doesn't this remind you of Cassie Marlowe?" She gestured to the body, aware of how her next words might sound. "The positioning, it's almost identical. I think we're looking at a serial killer."

"I—I think I heard her name on the news," Morales said, frowning, "but I don't really know the case."

Clara pulled out her phone, quickly running a search and pulling up images of Cassie's crime scene to show him.

Derek's brow creased with skepticism as he studied the images and then surveyed the scene before him. His instinct for reading human behavior was uncanny, but where Clara saw patterns and connections, Derek often sought tangible proof.

"I mean, there's definitely similarities, Clara. But the Marlowe case isn't our jurisdiction. And I don't think there's enough here for us to take it over."

"Look closer, Derek," Clara implored, her voice firm. "This isn't just my memory playing tricks. There's a deliberateness here that's hauntingly familiar. We need to follow this lead."

He exhaled, the mist of his breath visible in the cold air. For a moment, he said nothing, contemplating the silent figure before them. Then, with a reluctant nod, he conceded, "All right. Let's see what the coroner has to say about Marlowe's case. Maybe they'll be able to match the knife wounds or the angle of the kill. If there's any merit to your theory, that's our best shot at finding a connection."

Clara nodded, grateful for a partner who was willing to follow her lead even when the patterns weren't nearly as clear to him as they were in her mind's eye.

If she was right, this killer was trying to tell them something. And they needed to figure it out soon—before he took another victim and wrote another chapter in his sick, sadistic story.

CHAPTER FOUR

Clara Pike could feel the chill of the morgue seeping into her bones as she and Derek stepped through the stainless-steel doors. It wasn't just the refrigerated air; it was the solemnity that clung to the sterile walls, the tinge of death that no amount of antiseptic could ever quite erase. The overhead fluorescents buzzed faintly, casting a pallid light over the room, making the shadows retreat reluctantly into corners.

"Agent Pike, Agent Morales," Dr. Lisa Hammond greeted them, her voice echoing slightly in the quiet. She was the medical examiner tasked with unraveling the enigmas written on cold flesh, clad in a blue gown that did little to soften her austere appearance—a contrast to her warm, if weary, eyes. Her hands were steady and sure, a testament to years spent peeling back the layers of mystery shrouding the silent figures on her tables.

"Dr. Hammond," Clara acknowledged with a nod. She trusted this woman's findings almost as much as she trusted her own eyes, and right now, those eyes were searching, taking in every detail from the position of the instruments on the counters to the precise manner in which autopsy reports were stacked.

"Let's start with the preliminary findings for Cassie Marlowe," Hammond said, leading them toward a table where a body lay under a stark white sheet. The medical examiner pulled back the cloth, revealing a woman frozen in time, her skin an unnatural shade of pale against the silvery steel.

"The cause of death was the severing of the carotid," Hammond said, motioning to the neck. "The cut was quick and clean. The killer knew what he was doing."

"Her nails," Clara murmured, noting the broken edges and the skin beneath them. "She fought back."

"Indeed," Hammond confirmed. "But we couldn't get any DNA. Seems like he cleaned them afterwards."

"Countermeasures," Clara replied. "Either he's done this before…"

"Or he's watched a lot of crime shows," Hammond suggested. "It's hard to tell these days."

"Any sign of sexual assault?" Derek asked, his voice measured, yet Clara detected the undercurrent of disgust.

"None," Hammond replied. "But there's something else—the body was... posed? The killer didn't just leave her there. He cleaned the blood. Folded her hands after death."

"Staging," Derek concluded, his profiler's mind already sifting through the implications.

"Exactly," Hammond agreed. "There's a meticulousness here that doesn't seem consistent with a crime of passion. Plus, the efficiency of the method of death. The lack of any other knife wounds. It's almost as if the killer had a level of... I don't know. Care, perhaps?"

The revelation hung heavy between them, a grim tapestry woven with methodical intent. Clara felt the familiar tug at the edges of her consciousness, the need to connect, to understand. She thought of Jessica Hanley, the other victim, whose crime scene they had just left, and the gnawing suspicion that these two scenes were not just similar, but entwined.

"I need to see the crime scene photos," Clara stated, her voice resonating with an authority that left no room for argument.

Dr. Hammond nodded, understanding the necessity of the request, and moved to a side table where a folder lay, its contents a macabre collection of glossy images. She handed the folder to Clara, who opened it with methodical precision, laying out the photographs like tarot cards foretelling a dark future.

Each image was a frozen moment in time, a silent scream captured in pixels and ink. Clara's eyes darted over the pictures, absorbing every detail with her uncanny knack for observation. The arrangement of the auditorium, the position of the body, the pattern of the wound—all danced in her mind, coalescing into a narrative only she could read. Derek watched her, his analytical mind trying to keep pace with her rapid-fire deductions.

"See?" Clara said to Derek, pointing at the angle of Cassie's head. "That and the hands. It looks an awful lot like the way Jessica Hanley was positioned." It wasn't proof, but it was a whisper of connectivity that echoed in the chilling expanse of the morgue.

Derek leaned closer, examining the photos. "They're definitely similar," he conceded, "but that doesn't necessarily mean the same person posed them. If we could match the weapon..."

Clara turned to Dr. Hammond, who shook her head.

"Hanley won't come to me. Not if it's a federal case. But if you want, I can ask to have her transferred here, or I can send all of my notes to your medical examiner."

"Thank you, Dr. Hammond," Derek replied. "We'll dig into this a bit further and be in touch."

Dr. Hammond nodded and returned to her work. As they exited the morgue, Clara turned her attention to Derek.

"You of all people know there are no coincidences in our line of work. This… these two murders are too similar."

Derek's skepticism lingered, but he couldn't ignore the conviction in Clara's voice or the analytical fire in her eyes. He had seen that look before—the same one that burned when she spoke of her brother's unsolved case. It was a mix of fierce determination and a desperate search for justice.

"Look, I hear you, but right now, we just have two bodies. There's variance in the victimology, variance in the type of locations. Folded hands and a similar method of death simply aren't enough for us to declare a serial yet.

"But," he murmured after a tense moment, "we can take another look at the Marlowe crime scene. See if there's anything there the pictures didn't capture. But we tread carefully, Clara. We can't afford to spook whoever did this. If they're watching, we don't want to let them know we've made the connection. If they are a serial, and they are trying to communicate something, thinking we're on to them might accelerate their timeline. Plus, we don't want to piss off local PD by seeming like we don't trust them to do their jobs."

"Agreed," Clara replied. "Thank you for trusting my instincts on this—at least enough to look further."

"Always," Derek replied as they stepped out into the parking lot. "I've known you long enough to know better than to ever dismiss your instincts out of hand. And besides, I do think you're right about the potential connection. I just don't want us leaping from speculation to conviction without proof."

"Of course."

"Now the more important question," Derek said with a smile that Clara already knew meant he was going to try to inject some levity into the situation. "Who's driving? You or me?"

Clara grinned as she held out the palm of her hand, and, in a practiced motion, Derek tossed her the keys.

***

The afternoon sun was high in the sky as they arrived at the school where Cassie Marlowe worked. The building stood before them, an edifice of faded grandeur and peeling paint. She could see the former beauty of the place, but decades of students running in and out had clearly taken its toll.

Clara stepped out of the car, the soles of her boots connecting with the ground in a decisive thud. She didn't bother to wait for Derek; her strides were quick and purposeful as she made her way to the entrance.

"Clara, wait," Derek called after her, but she was already pushing through the doors of the auditorium. The vast space opened up around her, rows of empty seats facing a stage that was once a platform for dreams but now served as a grim tableau.

Clara moved down the aisle, her eyes scanning every inch of the place. The somber silence was broken only by the sound of Derek's footsteps echoing behind her. As he caught up, he saw her crouch near the spot where Cassie Marlowe's body was found, examining the floorboards with meticulous attention.

"Find something?" Derek asked, watching Clara run her fingers along a barely discernible mark on the wood.

"Maybe," she murmured, tracing the faint outline. It was a small scuff, easily overlooked, but to Clara, it was a silent scream in the quiet of the auditorium. She rose to her feet, her mind racing as she pieced together the scant clues—the position of the body, the trajectory of blood spatter, the unseen dance of predator and prey that was played out in this tragic theater.

"Could be from a shoe or something dragged..." Clara trailed off, her thoughts branching into a hundred different possibilities. She turned her attention to the stage, its curtains drawn back just as they would have been on the night Cassie Marlowe died. There was an intimacy to the crime scene that unsettled Clara.

"Could also have been from any of the thousands of kids who've used this space over the years," Derek countered.

"Let's check the stage," Clara said, her voice echoing slightly in the cavernous room. Together, they ascended the steps, their movements deliberate, respectful of the hallowed ground of the investigation. The wooden planks of the stage groaned under their weight, as if protesting the intrusion.

Derek watched as Clara surveyed the area, her eyes sharp and discerning. He had seen her like this countless times—her gift for observation transforming her into a conduit for the silent stories that lingered in the aftermath of violence. She bent down again, this time picking up a splinter of wood that seemed out of place.

“Fragment from something… Could be significant,” she mused, rolling the piece between her fingers with a forensic tenderness. Derek knew better than to interrupt; Clara was in her element, the whispers of the past growing louder as she tuned into the frequency of the crime scene.

“Remember, we’re looking for connections,” he reminded her gently, not wanting to break her concentration but needing to anchor her to the task at hand.

Clara nodded, her expression solemn. “I know,” she replied, her gaze still locked on the stage. “And I’m certain they’re here. We just have to listen closely enough.”

“Maybe if we spoke with one of her co-workers?” Derek suggested. “Might help us get some additional perspective.”

“Good idea.” Clara nodded. “Lead the way.”

Clara’s boots clicked against the polished linoleum of the school corridor, a rhythm that matched the pounding of her thoughts, as she and Derek made their way through the maze of hallways that branched off the auditorium. Her eyes flitted over the colorful bulletin boards and lockers adorned with magnets and stickers—a stark contrast to the grim reason for their visit.

“Can I help you?” A voice sliced through the academic stillness, drawing Clara out of her reverie.

“Perhaps,” Clara said, pivoting toward the source—a middle-aged man wearing a custodian’s uniform, his face creased with lines of both care and age.

“We’re investigating the murder of Cassie Marlowe,” Clara explained, her tone deliberate yet compassionate. “We understand she was an employee here.”

“Ah, yes, Miss Marlowe…” The man’s eyes dimmed, the fondness in his voice tinged with sorrow. “Such a tragedy. She was one of our best. The kids loved her.”

“I’m sure,” Derek replied.

“You know, she went to school here, too,” the man added. “All the way, K to twelve. She was a real success story until… well, you know.” He sighed heavily, the weight of the loss evident in the sag of his shoulders.

“Did she have any enemies? Anyone who might have—” Derek began, but the man interjected before he could finish his sentence.

“Cassie? Heavens no. She was the very definition of beloved. I’ll never understand what would make a person do something like that to someone like her.”

"Thank you for speaking with us," Clara said, offering a polite nod before turning away, her thoughts churning. She thought about the fact that Cassie grew up in this same institution and was struck by how poignant that detail seemed—Cassie's life coming full circle within these walls. A beginning and an end.

"Clara?" Derek's voice pulled her back to the present. "You alright?"

"Fine," she murmured, though her furrowed brow betrayed her inner turmoil.

"Let's walk the perimeter one more time," she suggested, her gaze revisiting the auditorium doors. They moved in tandem, tracing the edges of the taped-off area where Cassie's body had been discovered.

The silence enveloped them as they scrutinized the vacant space, but to Clara, it was anything but empty. Shadows clung to the corners like specters, whispers of the past clinging to the dust motes that danced in the slanting light. Each step they took seemed to stir the echoes of the room's history, the laughter and tears of countless students—and now, the silent scream of a life violently ended.

As her gaze scanned the vastness of the auditorium once more, the crime scene photos flashed through her mind, each image imprinted with laser precision thanks to her photographic memory. The position of Cassie's body, the eerie similarity to Jessica's murder—it all swirled together in a maelstrom of clues and questions. It allowed Clara to see things Derek couldn't, but it also made it far easier for her to get overwhelmed.

She closed her eyes for a moment, willing the barrage of images to stop just long enough for her to focus.

"Two women, two lives cut short," Clara spoke softly, almost to herself. "There has to be a link, some thread connecting them beneath the surface."

"Think it's personal?" Derek asked, watching her closely.

"Could be," she conceded, her intuition gnawing at her. "But it's deeper than that. This isn't random; it's methodical, calculated. And whatever the connection is, it's the key to unraveling this whole twisted tapestry."

"Then we'll find it," Derek stated firmly, his resolve steeling her own.

"Yes," Clara affirmed, her eyes reflecting a steely determination. "We have to."

As they exited the auditorium, Clara knew one thing for certain—their investigation was far from over. The shadows of the past were beckoning, and she would follow them wherever they led, no matter how deep into the darkness they might take her.

CHAPTER FIVE

As they drove away from the auditorium, Clara took in the cityscape unfurling outside their unmarked car, the unexpected rain smearing the world into a watercolor of urban melancholy, the skyline a jagged rhythm against the overcast canvas.

"Back to headquarters?" she asked Derek.

"I had a different thought," Derek offered. "Look, I get it," he continued, gripping the steering wheel with an assuredness that somehow seemed at odds with the uncertainty clouding his eyes. "Your hunches are usually spot-on, and I'm inclined to think you're right here, too. There's a good chance these cases probably are linked. But right now, our primary job is to investigate Jessica Hanley's murder. That's the case we were assigned. And if we find something concrete linking it to local PD's, then—"

"Then we can make a move," Clara finished for him, knowing he was right even as the frustration coiled tighter within her. "Okay, so let's focus on Jessica Hanley. Anywhere in particular you want to start?"

"I was thinking maybe we could start with her sister. She might be able to give us a deeper understanding of Jessica than we could get from the case file."

"Yeah, I like that idea," Clara replied.

The decision settled between them like a truce, and Clara allowed herself a moment to absorb the possibilities. Derek had a way of grounding her when the threads of evidence tried to pull her in all directions; he was the compass to her map of memories and minute observations.

"I just keep wondering about the promenade where Jessica was killed," Derek said. "It's a weird spot to be so late at night—particularly a woman alone. It's a very high-risk behavior. And, if we are looking at the same guy who killed Cassie Marlow, a bizarre shift. It's rare to see someone go from low-risk victimology to high-risk instead of the other way around."

"Agreed," Clara admitted, her voice a soft echo of confusion. "But maybe her sister will help us understand."

Pulling up to the curb near the sister's building, they were greeted by the sight of a nondescript complex, its facade a mosaic of peeling paint and weathered bricks. It was a stark contrast to the vivid life Jessica once led. Clara stepped out of the car, her senses immediately cataloging every detail—the way the dying light caught on the droplets of rain clinging to the metal railing, the faint murmur of a television from behind a nearby window, the cloying scent of damp earth mingling with city grime.

The door to Jessica's sister's apartment loomed before them, an ordinary barrier between the world and the raw pain of loss that surely dwelled beyond.

Derek knocked, a series of measured taps that sounded too loud in the silence. Moments stretched into infinity until the door creaked open, revealing a woman whose reddened eyes and hollow cheeks bore the weight of fresh grief. Jessica's sister stood there, a ghostly shadow of the vibrant sibling lost, the remnants of tears streaking her face like rain over windowpanes.

"Rebecca Hanley?" Clara's voice was softer than she intended, imbued with an empathy born of shared suffering. "I'm Special Agent Clara Pike, and this is my partner, Special Agent Derek Morales. May we come in?"

Rebecca nodded mutely, stepping aside to grant them entry. Her apartment was a canvas of sorrow, with personal effects that whispered of happier times now overshadowed by the shroud of mourning.

"Thank you," Clara murmured, scanning the living room with eyes that missed nothing—the discarded tissues, the framed photographs, the half-empty cups of coffee.

"Can I get you anything?" Rebecca asked, her voice brittle as autumn leaves.

"No, thank you," Clara declined gently.

"We appreciate your willingness to speak with us," Derek offered.

"Of course," Rebecca replied, motioning meekly to the living room. "Please, make yourselves comfortable."

Clara positioned herself on the edge of a threadbare sofa, its fabric worn by time and touch. The air was heavy with silence, punctuated only by the occasional distant siren that reminded them of the city pulsing beyond these walls. Derek took a stance near the bookshelf, his eyes scanning titles and trinkets.

"Ms. Hanley," Clara began, her voice steady despite the churn of her thoughts, "we need to ask you some questions about Jessica. Could you tell us about her routine, her friends, anyone who might have held a grudge?"

Rebecca wrapped her arms around herself, as if bracing against a chill only she could feel. "Jess was… vibrant, loving. She made friends easily," she said, her gaze drifting toward a photograph of Jessica, smiling radiantly from behind glass. "She worked long hours, but she loved what she did—graphic design, it was a real passion for her. And her colleagues—they were like family."

"Did she ever mention anyone new in her life? Someone she met recently who stood out?" Clara probed, watching for any flicker of recognition or distress that might unfurl across the woman's features.

"Jess kept to her circle mostly. She never mentioned feeling unsafe or worried about anyone." Her fingers tensed around her own sleeves, knuckles whitening.

"Thank you," Clara acknowledged, noting the protective gesture, the subtle defenses rising like barricades. "It's important we understand her movements leading up to…"

Her sentence trailed off as Derek interjected, his tone deliberate, carrying a weight that seemed to compress the very air around them. "We found her at the old promenade at

Chesapeake and Ohio Canal National Historical Park. Did she frequent that area by any chance?"

Surprise flickered over Rebecca's face, a crack in her carefully maintained composure. "The promenade? Jessica wouldn't have—" She shook her head, confusion etching lines into her forehead. "That place… she hadn't gone there for years. Not since—"

"Since what?" Clara asked, leaning forward, sensing the precipice upon which they now teetered—a clue, a memory, something vital poised to tumble forth.

"Since college. It held bad memories for her," she replied, voice faltering. "After everything that happened there, I can't imagine why she'd go back."

"I'm sorry for prying, but memories of what, exactly?" Clara asked.

"Her ex," Rebecca replied. "They were high school sweethearts. Used to go to that promenade together all the time. And then, just before graduation, he took her out there one last time. Clara thought he was taking there to propose, but instead, he told her he was ending things. He'd met some other girl and was following her to Europe."

Derek exchanged a glance with Clara, an unspoken dialogue passing between them. Both understood the significance of such a location—it was either a message, or the echo of a past that refused to stay silent.

"Do you think the ex could have had anything to do with her murder?" Derek asked.

"No, last I heard he was living in Germany. Happy, with a wife and two kids. Plus, it's been like six years. There just wouldn't be any reason for him to come back now—not after all this time. But it is weird it happened at the promenade. I can't fathom what she would have been doing there. Especially at night. Jessica, she liked to have fun, but she wasn't the sort to take unnecessary risks."

"Thank you, Ms. Hanley," Clara said softly, the words a gentle tether pulling them back from the brink of revelation. "This information is very helpful. If you think of anything else, please let us know."

As they left the apartment, the air felt heavier, as though the building itself bore the weight of secrets untold. Clara's mind raced with questions. What force could compel someone to revisit a place of such heartache? Was it nostalgia, manipulation, or something more sinister? The answer lay hidden within the shadows of the old promenade, and Clara felt the familiar thrill of the hunt—the relentless pursuit of truth in the darkest of corners.

CHAPTER SIX

"Two victims," Clara started, her eyes locked on the landscape speeding past them as they headed back to FBI headquarters. "Both are tied to a location that resonates with them personally. That can't be a coincidence." Each word was weighted with the gravity of her theory—a theory she knew held water even if Derek wasn't ready to dive in.

"Clara, there's something to be said for personal connection, sure," Derek acknowledged, grabbing a sip of cold coffee from the tumbler in the console. "But we've seen it before—wrong place, wrong time. It might not be the work of a serial."

"Except Jessica's sister said that place held painful memories. Painful memories are intimate, Derek." Clara tapped a finger to her temple, as if accessing her own vault of memories. "This killer knows them, knows what will hurt them and where. They're staging retribution scenes."

Derek's brow creased with skepticism. "Intimate knowledge doesn't always point to a pattern, though. And besides, no one said anything about Cassie's memories at the school being painful. They were both connected to their locations, but Cassie worked at the school. She could easily have been a victim of opportunity. And frankly, so could Jessica. The fact that she had an emotional connection to the place could have just been a coincidence."

"This feels orchestrated, deliberate," Clara challenged, her gaze now shifting to meet his.

"Alright, but let's say you're correct," Derek replied, his voice tempered with reason. "If this is a serial, what's the common thread? What's driving them?"

"Isn't that the question of the hour?" Clara exhaled, taking a sip of her coffee.

"More like the question that keeps me up at night," Derek murmured, half to himself.

"Then let's agree on this," Clara pushed, her tone more insistent now. "We need to establish not only who would want to hurt these women but who would display them like this."

"Agreed," he conceded, finally meeting her intensity. "But we'd be remiss to tunnel-vision into one theory without considering all possibilities. You know how these cases go."

An uneasy silence settled over them; Derek's skepticism was a familiar counterpoint to her acute intuition. Clara knew that beneath his caution lay a shared urgency—a drive to unravel the twisted narrative entwined within the stark facts of their case.

Thankfully, despite the notorious nightmare that is DC traffic, Clara and Derek made the trip back relatively quickly, and it wasn't long before they were back at FBI headquarters. The fluorescent lights overhead hummed a steady, grating tune as Clara Pike's boots clicked against the gleaming floor.

She adjusted her credentials at her hip, a small gesture that grounded her in the reality of her task. The sprawling office was abuzz with activity—a hive of agents and analysts, each engrossed in their own puzzles. But for Clara, all that existed were the two women whose lives had been brutally severed.

She settled into her workspace, a sparse desk adorned only with the necessary tools of her trade. The screen before her flickered to life, casting a cold glow upon her features, and she dove into the digital remnants of lives taken too soon.

The first victim, Cassie, had an online presence that was both vibrant and haunting. Clara sifted through years of pictures and status updates, noting the places tagged, the friends who commented, the patterns of behavior. Her place of employment featured frequently—usually in photos or posts about her students, some of which featured the auditorium where her body was found.

The second victim, Jessica, appeared more reserved in her digital footprint. Clara combed through Jessica's profiles, the posts less frequent, the information less forthcoming. But there, among the innocuous photos of sunsets and coffee cups, was a clue. The promenade where Jessica's body had been discovered was featured several times. It was not just a background—it was a focal point in her older posts.

Could it be mere coincidence? Or did the killer find these locations on their social media accounts and then choose them to amplify their message, whatever twisted gospel they sought to preach?

Clara leaned back in her chair, eyes scanning the horizon of data one last time. Aside from their deaths, there was no direct link between the two women, no mutual friends or interactions that stood out. Yet, the significance of the chosen places was undeniable—a cruel and intimate knowledge of their lives exploited.

A shiver ran down Clara's spine as she pondered the implications. Someone was watching, waiting, and selecting their victims with a precision that spoke of a perverse intimacy. With every click, every scroll, Clara felt herself sinking deeper into the web of the unseen predator, her heart beating an erratic rhythm against the stillness of the room.

"Anything?" Derek asked.

"Connections are tenuous," Clara replied, her gaze never leaving the screen. "But I'm certain there's something here. They both had photos on their profiles taken at the places where their bodies were found."

"Keep digging," he urged, looking over at her with a furrowed brow. "There has to be a reason we're missing."

"Trust me," Clara said, a hint of steel lining her words, "I'll find it."

"Cross-referencing property records now," Derek said. His eyes were fixed on his screen, the reflection painting ghostly lines over his hardened features. He had always been the one to anchor their investigations in the tangible world, chasing down leads grounded in reality, while Clara delved into the psyche and secrets of their subjects.

Derek's gaze flitted from one document to another, spreadsheets and reports cascading before him as he sought a connection between the school and the promenade. The two victims, linked by death, seemed to have led lives that ran parallel but never intersected. He tapped into city planning archives, business permits, anything that might reveal a shared element between those two spots of sorrow.

"Hey, Clara," Derek called out, his tone betraying a spark of revelation. "You might want to see this."

Clara approached, the air around them charged with anticipation. Derek pointed at a name that appeared on service rosters for both locations—a man named Victor Dunn. He was a custodian employed by a company contracted for sanitation and maintenance services at both the school and the promenade.

"Could be nothing," Derek cautioned, "but it's the first solid link we've found."

"Could be everything," Clara replied, her mind already racing with possibilities. Victor Dunn, a ghost in the background of their victims' last moments on earth, a shadow that now demanded illumination.

"Let's find out more about him," she said, already opening a search on the laptop. Derek nodded, the skepticism in his eyes giving way to the thrill of the chase.

Clara leaned forward, her fingers skating across the keyboard with a focused intensity as she accessed the national criminal database. The dim glow from her computer screen cast angular shadows across her face, highlighting the determination etched into her brow. Beads of sweat formed at her temple, not from the heat of the cramped office but from the pressure of unraveling a killer's thread.

"Come on," she muttered under her breath, coaxing the system to reveal its secrets faster. The cursor blinked in tandem with her pounding heart, each throb a reminder that time was slipping through their grasp like sand. And then it appeared—a rap sheet for Victor Dunn, detailing minor offenses that painted a picture of a man constantly at odds with society's rules. Trespasses, petty thefts, and one aggravated assault from over a decade ago. Nothing recent, but enough to cast a shadow of doubt.

"Take a look," Clara said, tilting the monitor so Derek could see. "Victor's no stranger to the wrong side of the law."

"Old news though," Derek observed, his eyes scanning the list. "Nothing here screams 'serial killer.'"

"Maybe not," Clara conceded, "but patterns can resurface. Desperation… opportunity… they make people do stupid things." Her thoughts were a whirlwind of profiling knowledge, trying to apply psychological theory to the grim facts before them.

The room seemed to shrink around them, the air thick with implication and unspoken fears. Victor had been hiding in plain sight, his criminal past a footnote that had gone unnoticed until now. Clara couldn't shake the feeling that they were on the verge of something monumental.

"But this. This is something," Derek said, tapping at another file he'd pulled up on his tablet. "A complaint lodged against Victor Dunn just a few weeks ago by none other than Cassie Marlowe. She accused him of inappropriate behavior—and the company determined there was enough merit there to get him transferred out of the school."

"So he knew her? And he used to clean the school auditorium where we found her body?" Clara's voice was a whisper, barely audible above the hum of fluorescent lights.

"Exactly," Derek confirmed. "He got moved to the promenade after that."

"Where Jessica was found," Clara finished, connecting the dots with a chilling clarity. The coincidence was too stark to ignore. Each woman had crossed paths with Victor at a place of personal significance, a place where their lives had eventually ended.

"Could be our guy was holding a grudge," Derek pondered aloud, his skepticism waning in the face of mounting evidence. "At least against Cassie Marlowe."

"Or seeking some twisted form of retribution," Clara added darkly. Her gaze returned to the screen, her mind piecing together the jagged edges of Victor's profile. A custodian, seemingly invisible to those around him, yet privy to the intimate details of his victims' lives.

"Why Jessica, though?" Derek asked.

"Who knows. Maybe, after Cassie, he just got a taste for it."

"Let's bring him in," Derek said, and Clara felt her heart beat faster.

The suspense hung between them, a tangible thing that filled the stale air of the FBI office. They were close, closer than ever to catching a killer, and Clara felt the weight of that responsibility settle upon her shoulders like an iron mantle.

CHAPTER SEVEN

The killer sliced through his medium-rare tenderloin steak with a meticulousness that matched the precision of a surgeon. Each cut was deliberate, each bite a calculated movement as he chewed thoughtfully in the dimly lit dining room of his nondescript apartment. The only light emanating from the room was the eerie glow of multiple computer screens perched on a large desk, casting long shadows that danced across the walls and ceiling.

The chorus of muffled voices coming from the computers provided a sinister soundtrack to his solitary meal. With every forkful of food, his gaze oscillated between the screens, absorbing the words being spoken in the therapy sessions playing out before him. His eyes were sharp, analytical, dissecting every sentence, every quiver in their voices, seeking the fractures in the facades of those who bared their souls to the unseen therapist.

It hadn't been easy, planting the bugs. He'd had to endure dozens of hours spent in sessions pretending to care, pretending to want to get better, before he finally got the opportunity. The doctor kept pushing him, asking inane questions about his childhood. His mother.

The doctor thought he could help the man heal. He'd never understood. The killer didn't need healing. He *was* the healer. He understood what the doctor didn't—that talking would never heal anyone's problems. They needed to confront them. To face their trauma head-on. That was the only way they could ever truly be released from their pain. To do anything different was to squander their lives and potential entirely.

His dinner plate, a once-artistic arrangement of greens and reds, was now tainted with the dull sheen of meat juices, creating an abstract painting that seemed oddly fitting for the moment. His apartment was spartan; the furniture functional but devoid of personality, much like the man himself. It was a place of necessity rather than comfort, a base for his operations rather than a home.

Each recorded session was a window into vulnerability, a peek into the hidden depths where secrets lay buried. He'd gathered them meticulously, tapping into the digital stream of confessions with an ease that came from years of navigating cyber labyrinths. To anyone else, these files would have been an ethical breach, a gross violation, but to him, they were the key to understanding—no, correcting—the flaws in these individuals' narratives.

As the sounds of cathartic revelations filled the room, the air grew thick with an unspoken tension, a sense of foreboding that clung to the fabric of the curtains and settled like dust on the cold, hard floor. Here, surrounded by the disembodied admissions of pain and fear, he found a perverse solace, a dark corner of the world where his purpose was reaffirmed with every click of the mouse.

Finishing his meal, he pushed the plate aside, the remnants of his dinner as forgotten as the people on the screens once they ceased to serve their purpose. His focus sharpened, the soft clatter of cutlery replaced by the clicking of a computer mouse as he paused and replayed certain segments, leaning in closer when a particular phrase or emotion sparked his interest.

The atmosphere in the room was charged with the electricity of potential, of plans yet to unfold, and the hunger for what was to come. Silence fell for a brief moment as one recording ended and another began, the transition marked by the soft hum of machinery—a heartbeat in the stillness. He sat back in his chair, the observer in the shadows, watching and waiting as the dance of death continued on the screens before him.

His fingers danced across the keyboard with an almost tender grace, each tap another step deeper into the macabre ballet that held him enraptured. The glow from the screens cast a pallid light over his features, shadows playing upon the contours of his face as if they were reluctant to reveal too much about the man behind the monster.

On one screen, Cassie Marlowe's image flickered, her soft voice floating through the speakers like a ghostly whisper. She spoke of the loss of a childhood friend, a pain nearly two decades old and yet still incredibly fresh. He watched, his eyes never wavering from her face, as if he sought to memorize every line of pain that crossed her brow, every flicker of sadness in her deep brown eyes. Cassie, who had dedicated her life to nurturing young minds, had been unable to nurture her own wounded spirit.

Adjacent to Cassie's digital confessional, Jessica "Jess" Hanley recounted her own tale of despair. With fiery red hair cascading around her shoulders, she revealed the agony of love lost, the promenade where dreams turned to dust and promises became as hollow as the night was long. She laughed—a short, rueful sound—deriding her naivety, yet it was the undercurrent of enduring heartache that captured his attention.

In these intimate revelations, he found validation. He saw himself as an arbiter of emotional reckoning, forcing confrontation between his victims and their darkest memories. They must face their past, he reasoned, confront and embrace the agony before they could be freed from it. And then, they must be punished—put to death for wasting their lives reliving their trauma instead of ever moving forward. It was a twisted form of salvation, one that only he could deliver.

The ominous silence of the space was punctured only by the sounds of confession and the steady clicking of a mouse. Here, within this chamber of secrets and suffering, he felt more alive than anywhere else in the world. He leaned forward, eyes narrowing slightly as he replayed a segment of Cassie's session, dissecting her words, searching for the moment her voice broke, the instant the dam of her composure giving way to raw, unfiltered emotion. That was the moment he thirsted for—the pure, unadulterated truth of trauma.

He replayed Cassie's final moments in his mind's eye now, the fear that had glazed her eyes, the tremble in her voice as she begged for mercy. Her pleas echoed in his mind, not cries of desperation but rather whispers of vindication. He savored them like a connoisseur, each note of terror a testament to his power to force confrontation with a past that had been buried deep within her heart. Jessica's end was no less satisfying; her realization of the inevitable truth unfolding just as he had orchestrated. Their deaths were not merely the cessation of life but the culmination of their haunted histories, meticulously executed by his hand.

The room around him seemed to breathe in sync with his recollections. Books on forensic psychology, criminal profiling, and the darkest corners of the human psyche lined the shelves—each one a brick in the fortress of knowledge he had built around himself. He fancied himself not just a killer but an architect of absolution, guiding his victims through a labyrinth of their own making until they reached the center—their deepest pain—and there he would set them free before ending it all.

As he basked in the afterglow of his morbid triumphs, a new screen beckoned. Naomi Watson's visage filled the frame, her blonde hair like spun gold against the sterile backdrop of the therapist's office. She spoke of her fascination with history, the way she found solace in the stories of those long gone. But beneath her scholarly intrigue, there lurked a shadow—a childhood memory tethered to the old historic library that had once nearly claimed her life in its fiery demise.

He watched her, fixated. Each gesture, every inflection of her voice, was cataloged, analyzed, a puzzle demanding to be solved. Here was a woman whose trauma was intertwined with the very fabric of her identity. Just his type.

His fingers drummed lightly on the tabletop, anticipation curling at the edges of his thoughts. Naomi's time was coming, another chapter waiting to be written in the macabre narrative he authored. He relished the idea of bringing her full circle, back to the charred remains of her sanctuary turned inferno. There was a poetic justice in it, a symmetry that appealed to his twisted sense of order. Yes, he thought, Naomi would confront her past, and in doing so, she would meet her end—a storybook conclusion to the tale he had woven from the strands of her darkest day.

His pulse quickened, a symphony of anticipation played out beneath his skin as the cursor hovered over the play icon. He could almost taste the metallic tang of excitement that tingled at the edge of his senses. Each murder had been an act of liberation, a way to force his victims to confront the very essence of their fears before snuffing them out like candles at the end of a vigil. Naomi was no different; she would be his next vessel of catharsis, and the thought sent ripples of illicit pleasure through his veins.

The room around him was awash in the dim glow of monitors, casting long shadows across the walls. A veritable nest of technology hummed quietly, each screen a window into the psyches of unsuspecting souls. As he sat there in the half-light, he felt like a puppet master in his den of digital voyeurism, each recording a string tethered to the lives he'd chosen to entangle with his own.

His plan for Naomi was coming together beautifully—a dark homage to her past. As he mulled over the details of what was to come, a cruel smile cut across his face, the kind that never quite reached his eyes.

Shaking off the fervor of his thoughts, he reached for his phone, its sleek surface cold and impersonal in his hand. With practiced ease, he unlocked the device and navigated to his messages. There she was, Naomi Watson—the unsuspecting lamb to his slaughter.

He scrolled through the text chain between them, though, of course, she didn't realize he was the man on the other end of the phone. As far as she knew, she was talking to her therapist, a man whose number he had spoofed. He'd been using it for weeks to convince her that she must confront the site of her greatest trauma. It had taken some doing, but she trusted him—or, at least, the man she thought he was, and that had allowed him to wear her down just enough to get what he needed.

"It's time, Naomi," he typed, his fingers deft on the touchscreen. "8:00 tonight."

He watched the typing bubble pop up and disappear. He couldn't risk her having second thoughts.

"You can do this," he added. "All our work has led up to this moment. And you want to get better, don't you?"

Again, the bubble popped up and stopped again. For a moment, he felt his gut twist with the possibility it had not worked. But then, there it was—the words he'd been waiting to hear.

"I'll be there."

CHAPTER EIGHT

Clara's eyes were steely as she watched her partner, Derek Morales, wrap up a phone call. On the other end of that call was the night shift manager for the cleaning company, who'd just confirmed that Victor Dunn was indeed on the schedule for the evening, set to make his rounds through the promenade where Jessica Hanley's life had been snuffed out just one night prior.

"Victor's coming," Derek said, his voice carrying a weight that seemed to pull the air from the room. "Any minute now."

A coil of anticipation tightened in Clara's gut. They couldn't afford to waste any time. With a swift motion, Clara was on her feet, her FBI badge glinting in the artificial light as she clipped it onto her belt next to her service weapon. Her mind raced over every square inch of the promenade, recalling the crime scene photos with vivid clarity.

"Let's go," Clara said, her voice firm, betraying none of the chaos of emotions roiling within her.

Derek gave a terse nod and followed Clara out the door, the urgency of their task propelling them forward. As they stepped into the cool evening air, the city's cacophony enveloped them, but the sounds fell away, muffled by the singular focus of their mission. The sky hung heavy with clouds that threatened rain, casting an ominous pall over the cityscape.

Derek's SUV sat at the curb, its black paint job blending into the night. The doors opened with a definitive thunk as they climbed inside, and the interior was immediately bathed in the soft glow of the dashboard lights. Derek gunned the engine to life, and the vehicle lurched forward into the stream of traffic.

As they weaved through the congested streets, Clara could feel the tension emanating from Derek beside her. She understood his unease; the profile they'd built of Victor Dunn painted him as unpredictable, a man whose quiet exterior might conceal volatile undercurrents. And Derek, with his innate understanding of the criminal psyche, likely sensed the danger Victor posed more acutely than anyone.

Turning her gaze to the window, Clara watched the buildings blur past, each one holding thousands of stories, most of which would never intersect with theirs. But tonight, one story mattered above all others—the story they hoped to conclude with Victor Dunn's apprehension.

The SUV maneuvered deftly through the labyrinthine streets, and soon, the familiar outline of the promenade came into view. Its wrought-iron arches stood like silent sentinels, guarding the memories of laughter and love, now overshadowed by tragedy.

"Almost there," Derek murmured, his hands tight on the steering wheel.

"Ready when you are," Clara responded, her tone steady despite the quickening of her pulse. This was it—the moment they'd been waiting for. Tonight, they would confront the man she hoped was responsible for both Jessica's and Cassie's deaths, bringing closure to their families once and for all.

The SUV's tires crunched over the gravel as Derek pulled into a parking space at the promenade. The last rays of the sun dipped behind the horizon, casting long shadows that melded with the growing darkness. Clara Pike stepped out, her boots making decisive sounds on the pavement like an audible punctuation to their urgent mission.

"Let's split up," she suggested, her eyes already scanning the territory—a hodgepodge of vendors and evening strollers milling about. "We'll cover more ground."

"Be careful," Derek replied, his voice carrying the weight of unspoken concern in the cool evening air.

Clara nodded, squaring her shoulders against the chill as she moved forward. The promenade, usually a mosaic of joyous activity, now felt like a macabre stage where every actor played a part in some sinister play. She weaved through the crowd, her gaze darting from face to face, searching for the one that matched the grainy photo they had of Victor Dunn.

She approached a group of workers gathered around a utility cart laden with cleaning supplies. "Excuse me," she began, her voice authoritative yet not unkind. "I'm looking for Victor Dunn. Is he around?"

A man with a name tag reading "Marty" glanced up from adjusting a mop handle. "Vic? Yeah, he should be on duty. Check by the fountain area. He starts his rounds there after sundown."

"Thank you," Clara said, giving him a curt nod before heading toward the fountain, her senses heightened. She found the splashing water from the ornate stone structure almost deafening, filling the space with a constant, thrumming background noise that made it difficult to focus.

As Clara drew closer, her eyes locked onto a solitary figure hunched over a trash bin, a long-handled broom in hand. His movements were methodical, almost ritualistic, as if each sweep of the broom was a carefully considered stroke on a larger canvas.

"Victor Dunn?" Clara called out tentatively, stepping closer. The man straightened slowly, turning to face her, and in the dim light, his features became clear. This was the man whose presence at both crime scenes was more than mere coincidence. This was the man who might hold the answers to questions that had haunted them for far too long.

"Can I help you?" he asked, his voice betraying no emotion, his face an unreadable mask.

"Mr. Dunn, I'm—" Clara started, but at that moment, a siren wailed in the distance, slicing through the murmur of the crowd and causing Victor to flinch ever so slightly. Clara knew that flinch was an indicator. Victor likely had anxiety around the idea of law enforcement, which meant he might be a runner. Or inclined to get violent. Or both.

Clara Pike's heart throbbed in her ears, the adrenaline surging as she watched Victor Dunn's face contort from detached curiosity to panic as he spotted Clara's sidearm. "FBI," she announced firmly, stepping into his line of sight, badge held high like a talisman that could ward off evil—or in this case, deter flight.

"Victor Dunn, we need to talk to you about—" Derek started, quickly appearing at Clara's side, but his words were cut off by the sudden clatter of the broom hitting the ground.

Victor's eyes darted from Clara to Derek and then to the space between them, calculating, assessing. Then, with the explosive urgency of a startled prey, he bolted—a blur of desperation that cut through the thick tension.

"Stop!" Clara commanded, even as her legs powered into motion, her training kicking in seamlessly. Her gaze, sharp as a hawk's, tracked every movement Victor made, recording each detail—the way his left arm swung wider than his right, the slight limp that betrayed an old injury.

The promenade was a labyrinth of shadows and light, the streetlamps casting an eerie glow on the uneven cobbles. Tables from nearby restaurants spilled onto the walkway, chairs haphazardly pushed back as patrons turned to look at the commotion. Victor weaved between them with surprising agility, knocking over a chair that clattered loudly behind him to try and keep Clara and Derek at bay.

Clara's photographic memory mapped their surroundings in real-time, predicting Victor's most likely path even as she navigated the obstacles. Her lungs burned with exertion but she pushed harder.

Derek was close on her heels, his own determination a palpable force. She knew without looking that his jaw would be set in that familiar, resolute line, his profiler's mind already trying to anticipate Victor's next move.

People shouted, their evening disrupted by the pursuit, some jumping out of the way, others frozen in place. A waiter balancing a tray of drinks narrowly avoided a collision, sending glasses clinking precariously as he sidestepped the chaos.

"Watch out!" Clara barked at a young couple who had stepped into their path, her voice cutting through the din. They scrambled back just in time, eyes wide with shock as the agents rushed past.

Ahead, Victor shoved through a group of teenagers, their laughter turning to exclamations of surprise. The gap between them was closing; Clara could almost reach out and touch him, but Victor wasn't giving up easily.

He vaulted over a low wall, landing awkwardly but continuing his desperate sprint. Clara followed suit, feeling the jolt in her knees as she hit the ground running.

Just a little further, she urged herself, pushing through the fatigue that threatened to slow her steps. She kept her focus laser-sharp, her eyes tracking Victor's movements with predatory precision. She cataloged the subtle shift of his shoulders as he prepared to change direction, the slight stumble on uneven cobblestone, the frantic glance over his shoulder that told her he knew they were gaining ground.

Suddenly, Victor broke free from the confines of the promenade, bursting onto the street. Clara and Derek followed in tandem, their own safety cast aside as cars honked and swerved. Headlights illuminated their path, casting long shadows that seemed to chase them just as fervently as they pursued Victor.

The street was a gauntlet, and Victor a cornered animal darting through the danger. But Clara was relentless. Ahead, Victor's stamina waned, his movements growing sluggish. Clara could sense the shift in momentum, could almost taste the impending capture. And then it happened—Derek lunged with athletic grace, tackling Victor to the pavement with a force that expelled the air from the suspect's lungs in a single whoosh.

"Victor Dunn, you are under arrest," Clara declared, her voice steady despite the surge of her pulse. As she recited his rights, the words felt like a solemn chant, a necessary incantation to keep the darkness at bay. "You have the right to remain silent. Anything you say can and will be used against you in a court of law..."

On the cold asphalt, Victor lay defeated, the chase at an end. This was one piece of the puzzle locked into place. Yet, as she looked down at Victor, Clara couldn't shake the feeling that this was just the beginning. She braced herself for what was yet to come, the ominous weight of the unknown pressing down upon her like the fog rolling in from the sea.

CHAPTER NINE

The interrogation room was a cold, sterile cube, its walls a suffocating shade of gray. The only sound was the low hum of the air conditioning mingling with the faint buzz of fluorescent lights overhead. Clara sat across from Victor Dunn, her gaze locked on his. She took in every detail—the way he hunched his shoulders defensively, the nervous twitch of his left eye, the jittery tap of his fingers on the steel table.

Victor Dunn, with his gaunt frame and unkempt beard that did little to hide his anxious expression, looked more like a cornered animal than the broody custodian whose employment put him at the center of their investigation. As they sat, the room itself seemed to close in around them, tight and oppressive, much like the circumstances that had forced this confrontation.

"Whatever you think I've done," Victor's voice broke the silence—a raspy, defiant tone, "I didn't do it." His eyes darted between Clara and Derek, seeking an ally where there was none.

Clara leaned forward slightly, elbows on the table, hands clasped together. Her mind raced, images flashing behind her eyes. A promenade bustling with life, then chaos as Victor ran, desperate to escape. The look of surprise when Derek tackled him, the flash of handcuffs. Why run if he wasn't guilty? But she couldn't ask that—not yet. This was a dance, and timing was everything.

"Is that so?" Clara's voice was even, betraying nothing of the whirlwind in her head. The game was on, and she played her part: the impassive federal agent, probing for truth amid layers of deceit. She observed Victor's response, another piece added to the mental mosaic she was assembling.

Derek Morales sat beside her, silent but observant. His dark eyes flicked back to Victor, reading the suspect as only a seasoned profiler could. Derek's presence was both reassuring and unsettling. They had been through this routine countless times, each knowing the other's moves. Yet Clara could feel the weight of Derek's trust issues pressing down on them, as palpable as the tension in the room.

Victor shifted in his seat, arms crossed in a defensive posture. "You've got the wrong guy," he insisted, a hint of desperation creeping into his voice. There was something else there too—fear, perhaps, or maybe indignation. Clara couldn't quite place it.

She remained silent, letting the moment stretch out, watching Victor squirm. Every second that ticked by, every bead of sweat that formed on Victor's brow, was data to be analyzed. She knew that patience often yielded more than pressure. In the stillness of the room, under the stark light, Clara could almost hear the cogs turning in Victor's head, calculating his next move. The silence was a tool, and she wielded it expertly, waiting for Victor to fill it with something—anything—they could use.

But Victor resisted. He'd clearly been in this situation before. Clara could see his anxiety mounting, but no matter how long she waited, he refused to say anything. He was smarter than she had given him credit for. He knew better than to give in to the trap of speaking first just to break the silence.

She was going to need a different tact.

"Victor," she began, her tone even but authoritative, "if you had done nothing wrong, there would have been no reason to run." The sentence lingered in the cramped space, a challenge hung between them.

Victor's eyes darted around the room, avoiding Clara's unwavering gaze. He licked his lips nervously, the fluorescent lights overhead casting harsh shadows across his face. His shoulders hunched slightly, as if trying to ward off the weight of her words.

"Running only makes sense if you're trying to escape something," Clara continued, her voice steady and calm. Her mind cataloged every twitch, every shift of Victor's body language. She could almost see the gears turning behind his anxious eyes, the mental calculations of risk versus reward. It was a game of chess, but Clara knew the board better than anyone. She had seen this dance before, the delicate push and pull of giving just enough rope for the suspect to hang himself with his own narrative.

The room's stark sterility—a single window with blinds shut tight, the humming buzz of the lone light fixture—felt like a world away from the vibrant chaos of the promenade where they had caught Victor. Here, in this boxed-in reality, there were no distractions, no crowds to melt into—only the truth, whatever it might be, waiting to be unearthed.

After what seemed an eternity, Derek broke the silence that had settled over them. His voice was low but firm, cutting through the tension like a knife. "Let's talk about Cassie Marlowe's murder."

Victor's reaction was immediate; his posture stiffened, and he seemed to retreat into himself, as if the very mention of Cassie's name had erected walls around him. Derek's comment was subtle yet incisive, the perfect follow-up to Clara's psychological groundwork. They were painting a picture piece by piece, and Victor's countenance betrayed his discomfort with the subject.

While Derek kept his gaze fixed on Victor, Clara studied the man before them with practiced scrutiny. She noticed the quick pulse at his neck, the way his hands clenched and unclenched beneath the table. Despite his palpable anxiety, the man remained an immovable object.

But then, something shifted. Perhaps they'd just waited long enough. Perhaps Victor had done the mental math and decided there was more to be gained from defending himself than remaining silent. Whatever the case, he opened his mouth slightly, and Clara felt a sense of relief wash over her. Finally, they were getting somewhere.

"Look." Victor's voice broke the silence, rough as gravel. "I didn't have anything to do with Cassie Marlowe. Yeah, I knew her. Didn't like her much, but that doesn't mean I'd kill her."

The air grew thick with his assertion, hanging between them like a noose waiting to tighten. Clara felt that instinctual tug at the back of her mind that came with years of dissecting lies from truth. She sat motionless, her gaze unwavering as she considered his words amidst the stark backdrop of the room—every surface clinical and untouched except for the disarray of Victor's presence.

"Victor," Clara began, her tone measured, "your history with Cassie, your clear dislike for her... It paints an unfortunate picture, especially considering you fled the moment Derek and I showed up at the promenade." She leaned forward slightly, her hands flat against the cool surface of the table. "Tell me, Victor. Do you have something against women generally, or was it just Cassie?"

The accusation seemed to reverberate off the white cinder block walls, each syllable a drumbeat heralding guilt. Clara watched as Victor's facade began to crack, his eyes now flickering with fear. Fear, she knew, could be a beacon of truth in a sea of deception.

The power in the room shifted palpably, with Clara holding the reins. As the seconds stretched on, the silence became an entity of its own, pressing down upon Victor with an intensity that seemed to demand a confession. Clara held her ground, her expertise in reading the room, the suspect, the situation—all coming to bear in this pivotal moment of confrontation.

Victor's eyes darted around the interrogation room, the stark fluorescence casting deep shadows across his gaunt face. His Adam's apple bobbed as he swallowed hard, a sheen of sweat now glistening on his forehead. Clara watched him closely, her gaze unyielding, as she sensed his resolve waning under the pressure of their scrutiny. The room felt tight with anticipation, the air thick with the scent of stale coffee and the faint tang of fear.

"Listen." Victor's voice cracked, his words tumbling out in a rush of desperation. "I—I ran because I had stuff on me, okay?"

"Stuff?" Derek asked.

"Drugs. Nothing major. Just a little bit of weed." Victor glanced at Derek, then back to Clara, seeking some semblance of understanding or perhaps mercy.

"I can't go back inside. Not again. And they'd violate my parole over that. That's why I ran. But you gotta believe me. Murder?" He shook his head vehemently, hands clenched into fists on the table. "That's not me."

Clara maintained her composure, though inside she felt a twinge of pity. She knew all too well the crippling grip of fear, how it could drive a person to the brink. But compassion had no place here—not yet.

"So you're saying you were more afraid of being caught with drugs than you were of us accusing you of murder?" Her question hung between them, an unspoken challenge.

"Exactly!" Victor exclaimed, relief momentarily flooding his features before the gravity of his situation seemed to crash upon him once more. "I didn't kill Cassie. I couldn't. Look, we had history, sure, but…" His voice trailed off into silence, leaving only the hum of the fluorescent lights above.

Taking a moment, Clara allowed the silence to swell, pressing down on Victor like a physical weight. She flicked her eyes toward Derek, giving a subtle nod, signaling him to take the lead.

Derek leaned forward, his presence commanding yet calm. "What about the night Cassie was killed? Where were you, Victor? Can anyone vouch for your whereabouts?"

"Alibi," Victor muttered, almost to himself, before raising his gaze to meet Clara's, a smile spreading across his face.

"I've got one. Airtight. I was at my sister's place, crashed on her couch. She'll tell you." His voice steadied as he presented this fragment of hope, a lifebuoy in the stormy sea of accusation. "And that girl they found this morning? I didn't know her, man. No motive."

“Alright, Victor,” Clara said, her tone even, betraying none of her skepticism. “We’ll check out your story. But remember, if you’re lying—” She let the threat hang, unfinished yet unmistakable.

Victor nodded, a ragged breath escaping him as he slumped back in his chair, the fight seemingly drained from him. Clara gave Derek a brief look, signaling the end of the interrogation. As they stood to leave, the heavy door creaking open, Clara couldn’t shake the feeling of frustration at the dead end they had reached.

The room emptied except for Victor, who sat alone with his thoughts, the ominous echo of the door slamming shut ringing in his ears. Clara paused outside, the coolness of the hallway seeping into her bones. She had hoped for a breakthrough, but instead, they were back to square one. With each passing moment, the killer remained at large, and the clock ticked inexorably forward.

CHAPTER TEN

Naomi's hand hovered over the weathered brass handle of the tall, arched doorway, her heart pounding a frantic rhythm that echoed the trepidation coursing through her veins. With a deep breath that did little to steady her nerves, she pushed open the door, the hinges protesting with a long, drawn-out creak that seemed to resonate within the hollow remnants of the old library. The scent of mildew and decay assaulted her senses, a stark contrast to the crisp, musty aroma of well-loved books that once filled the air. She stepped inside, her steps unsteady as the last rays of twilight fought to illuminate the ruins through broken windows and gaping holes in the walls.

The interior was a carcass of its former glory, the once majestic shelves now gnarled skeletons reaching out from the shadows. As she walked further into the abandoned remains of the library, Naomi could not help but recall the vibrant colors of the past; the rich mahogany that lined the walls in elegant panels, the deep reds and golds of the Oriental rugs that softened every footfall, the gilded spines of centuries-old tomes that whispered secrets of the ages to anyone who would listen. Now, all that remained were charred fragments scattered across the floor like fallen leaves in autumn, the paint on the walls blistered and peeling away to reveal the cold, unforgiving brick beneath.

Her eyes, tinged with the ghost of innocence, traced the outlines of what used to be an exquisite reading nook. There, amid the plush velvet cushions and the warm glow of a brass lamp, young Naomi had journeyed through realms of dragons and queens, of distant galaxies and undersea kingdoms. Her imagination had been set alight in this very spot, the stories fueling dreams that soared beyond the confines of her neighborhood. But now, the nook lay in ruin, the cushions rotted away, the lamp toppled and tarnished, its light extinguished forever.

The contrast between past and present was harrowing. Where there once stood a sanctuary for the curious and the learned, there was now only the husk of desolation. Naomi's footsteps echoed too loudly in the silence, a stark reminder of the life that had once thrummed within these walls. A lump formed in her throat as she thought of the eager young girl with golden locks and bright eyes who had raced through these aisles, hungry for the knowledge that each bound treasure promised. That girl seemed like a stranger now, separated by years and layers of ash that clung to Naomi's memory, each step forward a reluctant dance with the shadows of yesteryear.

Naomi inhaled sharply as her gaze flickered over the charred remnants of bookshelves, the blackened spines of books she once adored now crumbling into ash at the slightest touch. This place—her haven, her escape—had become a sepulcher of dreams long dead. The acrid scent of burnt paper and wood lingered stubbornly, a pungent reminder of the inferno that had nearly claimed her life.

As she moved deeper into the skeletal remains of the library, her fingers brushed against the scorched remains of a familiar balustrade, its intricate carvings forever lost to the ravages of flame. She remembered clinging to this very spot, her lungs screaming for air as smoke billowed around her like a malevolent specter. Panic had surged through her veins, an icy torrent that threatened to paralyze her even as she fought to break free from the conflagration's grasp.

The heat had been unbearable, a ravenous beast that consumed everything in its path. Naomi could still hear the desperate crackling of the fire as it devoured tome after tome, each one a guardian of knowledge succumbing to destruction. She had tried to hide from it, but that had only made things worse. The firefighters had gotten everyone out that they could see, but Naomi had hidden so well that they could not see her.

Her heart raced as the memory clawed at the edges of her mind, desperate to drag her back into the depths of that nightmarish blaze.

She could almost feel the blistering caress of flames against her skin, the terror of being ensnared with no hope of rescue. It was a memory etched into her very soul, a harrowing dance with death that had left its mark upon her in the form of both physical and emotional scars. Each step forward seemed to echo with the roar of the fire, a cacophony of despair that resonated with the creaks and groans of the decaying structure around her.

Naomi paused, closing her eyes for a moment as she struggled to anchor herself in the present. But the past was relentless, its tendrils weaving through her consciousness, threatening to pull her under. She could see herself, years younger, her face smeared with soot as she huddled beneath a table, the world around her alight with a ferocious hunger.

It took every ounce of her will to push those memories aside, to focus on the here and now rather than succumb to the haunting visions that sought to overwhelm her. This place was a tombstone commemorating a day that had forever altered the trajectory of her life, a stark monument to the fragility of existence. Yet, here she stood amidst the ruins, a testament to survival, even as the echoes of that fateful day whispered insidiously in her ear, promising to unmake her with their ghostly refrain.

Naomi's foot caught on an upturned tile, her balance faltering as she steadied herself against a charred bookshelf that groaned under the weight of her touch. The sudden jolt was enough—a spark igniting the powder keg of memories she had been desperately trying to keep at bay. Her breath hitched, ragged and sharp, as if inhaling the smoke anew, the acrid scent of burning paper and wood flooding her senses once again.

The library, once a sanctuary of whispers and quiet discovery, erupted into a cacophony of crackling flames in her mind. The heat wrapped around her like a suffocating blanket, and for a terrifying moment, Naomi was there, not here; then, not now. She could hear the screams of the other patrons and the voracious roar of the fire as it devoured everything in its path, feel the heat blistering her skin, see the ominous glow of the inferno reflecting in the terror-widened eyes of her younger self. Her heart raced, each beat a drumroll echoing the panic that had seized her all those years ago.

The ceiling beams groaned ominously overhead, mirroring the creaks from the past. The fire's tongues licked at the edges of her vision, the searing pain almost tangible. Naomi squeezed her eyes shut, willing the images away, but the darkness behind her eyelids served as a canvas for the blaze to paint its horrors anew. She was choking on the thick smoke, the yoke of fear clasping tight around her throat, the relentless heat threatening to consume her whole.

"Here," she whispered fiercely, prying her eyes open to let in the dim light of the present. "I'm here."

She sucked in a lungful of cool, musty air—so different from the scalding drafts that had once filled her lungs—and planted her feet firmly on the uneven ground. One by one, she catalogued the sensations anchoring her to the now: the cold bite of the metal shelf against her palm, the rough texture of her jeans against her legs, the distant sound of traffic muffled by the library's crumbling walls.

"Five things you can see," she muttered to herself, a grounding exercise her therapist had taught her to tether her to reality when the past loomed too large. Her gaze flitted across the ruined space, latching onto details—the jagged silhouette of broken windows, the moss creeping up stone pillars, the way the moonlight filtered through dust motes suspended in the air, the stark contrast of graffiti on ancient walls, the delicate web spun by a spider in the corner.

"Four things you can touch," she continued, pressing her fingertips against the cool, solid floor beneath her, the frayed fabric of her jacket, the small pebble she found by her shoe, the thin chain of her necklace—a talisman against the specters of memory.

"Three things you can hear." She focused on the soft whistle of wind through cracked masonry, the distant cry of a city bird, the faint rustle of leaves disturbed by her own movements.

"Two things you can smell." Naomi inhaled the damp earthiness of decay, the faint trace of rain from outside the walls.

"One thing you can taste." She ran her tongue over her lips, tasting the tang of fear still lingering but receding with each measured breath.

As each sensation grounded her further, the grip of the flashback loosened, the fiery hellscape receding into the corners of her mind where it belonged. The smoky tendrils dissipated, leaving behind the stark, silent reality of the ruins—a place hollowed out by disaster but no longer alight with her nightmares. Naomi stood alone amidst the remnants, the phantom agony of the blaze replaced by a growing sense of command over her own mind. The library held ghosts, yes, but she refused to become one of them. She was alive, here, now, and she would not surrender to the echoes of the past.

Naomi shuffled through the debris, her hands trembling as she picked her way across the fractured floor tiles, now cloaked in dust and ash. Her footsteps echoed, mocking the silence that had replaced the quiet whispers of page-turning and hushed conversations.

"Coming here… it's a step forward," she murmured to herself, attempting to stitch the fabric of her resolve tighter with each word. He'd promised her that coming here would give her closure. But the word felt foreign on her lips, a concept so distant it might as well have been a fairy tale.

Yet, somehow, the promise of understanding, of unraveling the knot that had tightened in her chest since the fire, seemed tangible here amongst the ruins. Still, even as she clung to that hope, it was a frail thread in the vast tapestry of her trepidation. This place was the origin of her nightmares, the epicenter of her darkest day, and to walk its hallowed halls was to dance with demons she'd long thought banished.

Her heart drummed a frantic rhythm against her ribs, each beat a thunderous reminder of the danger she had once escaped, and the peril that might yet lurk in the shadows. The sharp intake of her breath formed clouds in the chill air, coalescing into specters that swirled around her. The oppressive atmosphere of the library bore down on her, the weight of the past pressing against her shoulders, urging her to sink into the rubble and surrender to the despair that gnawed at the edges of her mind.

"Too much," she gasped, the walls seeming to close in around her. A whisper of panic unfurled within her chest, a silent scream that threatened to erupt and leave her exposed in the desolation.

She needed to escape, to find solace in the open sky and the relentless pace of the city beyond these cursed walls. The darkness seemed to pulse with a life of its own, a heartbeat syncing with her mounting fear. She cast a desperate glance over her shoulder toward the entrance, the streetlights there a lifeline in the encroaching gloom. With every fiber of her being straining toward that distant promise of safety, Naomi turned on her heel.

"Get out," she commanded herself, her voice barely a whisper, but it carried the weight of survival. She lunged toward the light, feet stumbling over the detritus that littered the ground, each step an eternity as she fought to reclaim the agency that this place sought to steal from her once more. The air grew thick, the musty scent of decay clawing at her throat and threatening to choke the courage that had brought her back to this forsaken relic of her past.

"Almost there," she encouraged herself, focusing on the exit, on the world outside where the past couldn't reach her, where the flames were just a memory, not a monster nipping at her heels. But as she drew closer, the threshold seemed to recede, as if the library itself was reluctant to release its grip on her soul.

Naomi's breath came in near-silent gasps, the sound muffled by the thick air and heavy silence of the dilapidated library. Her eyes, wide with a primal fear, darted frantically from shadow to shadow; every dark corner seemed to teem with the potential for danger. She could almost feel the press of unseen eyes watching her, waiting. The weight of the atmosphere was tangible, a suffocating blanket woven from decades of neglect and the ash of memories long since burned away.

A rat skittered across a fallen beam, its tiny claws scratching against the wood—a screeching herald to Naomi's frayed nerves. It was that small, mundane sound that broke the spell of the past's hold on her. Her head whipped around, heart hammering against her ribcage, seeking the source of the noise. But it wasn't the rodent's innocuous presence that stilled her blood—it was the sudden awareness of something far more sinister: the soft scrape of a shoe, a whisper of movement in the stillness behind her.

With the agility born of panic, Naomi spun on her heel, her gaze colliding with the murky void where light dared not penetrate. And then a silhouette materialized. It was an absence of light within darkness, a shape coalescing from the very shadows she had sought to evade.

Time constricted, seconds stretching into small eternities as Naomi faced the figure emerging from the void. Instinct screamed at her to flee, but her muscles were leaden, petrified by the haunting familiarity of this nightmare. Before she could marshal her limbs to respond, before her scream could claw its way up her throat, the figure lunged. A hand—solid, real, and terrifyingly human—clamped down on her shoulder with a vise-like grip.

Her breath hitched, caught between the reality of the attack and the icy tendrils of terror that wrapped around her spine. Naomi's mind, once so keen and vibrant among these same aisles now reduced to rubble, reeled under the assault. She could only stare, transfixed, as the stranger's other hand reached for her, the intent behind the motion as unreadable as the blank mask of shadow where a face should be. Then, contact—a second touch, cold and unyielding against her skin—and the world tilted on its axis as she was pulled inexorably into the dark embrace of the library's ruins.

CHAPTER ELEVEN

The last rays of the setting sun had long since abandoned the grim façade of the FBI headquarters, leaving it swathed in shadows that seemed to press against the glass with a palpable weight. Inside, fluorescent lights buzzed like an agitated swarm of insects as Clara gathered her belongings from her desk—a space now littered with crime scene photos and cryptic notes scrawled on sticky paper.

Her thoughts were a tumultuous sea, each wave crashing into the next: Victor Dunn's inscrutable gaze, her mother's unexpected call, the tangled web of her parents' separation. The chaos of her mind was mirrored by the disarray on her desk, but it was the one detail out of place—a pen carelessly left uncapped—that caught her attention and anchored her for a moment.

"Clara?" Derek's voice sliced through her reverie, jarring yet oddly comforting. She glanced up to find him standing in the doorway, his silhouette framed by the sterile light of the corridor. His eyes, shadowed and weary, still managed to convey a quiet strength that she found herself leaning on more often than not.

"Ready to call it a day?" he asked, the corners of his mouth lifting in a half-smile.

"Let's get out of here," Clara responded, her voice a mix of fatigue and resolve. She slipped her jacket over her shoulders, the leather creaking softly—a sharp contrast to the relentless hum of the office.

As they walked down the hallway together, their footsteps echoed off the linoleum, a staccato rhythm that seemed to resonate with the pulsing headache behind Clara's eyes. The walls were lined with framed commendations and somber portraits of agents past, each one watching them pass with silent scrutiny.

"Hey, before we head home," Derek said, breaking the silence as they approached the exit, "you want to grab something to eat? My treat."

The offer hovered between them, and for a brief moment, Clara hesitated. Her stomach churned at the thought of food, yet the gnawing emptiness reminded her that breakfast was a distant memory. She considered declining, yearning for the solitude of her apartment where she could untangle her thoughts without the burden of conversation.

But there was an undercurrent of concern in Derek's tone that she couldn't ignore—an acknowledgment of the lengthening shadows not just in the building, but within themselves.

"Sure," she finally said, with a small nod. "I could eat."

They pushed through the heavy doors, stepping out into the crisp evening air that hinted at the coming chill of night. As the door swung shut behind them, it seemed to seal away the remnants of the day's frustrations, if only for a moment.

Clara's shoes clicked methodically against the pavement, a subtle counterpoint to the murmuring city around them. The diner, perched on the corner of an otherwise nondescript block, cast a warm glow onto the sidewalk. It was a relic from another era, with its neon sign flickering fitfully in the gathering dusk. As they approached, the scents of grilling meat and onions wafted toward them, and Clara felt her stomach protest its neglect.

She paused for just a moment outside the glass door, peering through to the checkerboard tile floor and red vinyl booths that promised a certain nostalgia. Derek caught the brief hesitation, giving her a quizzical look.

"Second thoughts?" he asked, his voice tinged with the fatigue that shadowed both their faces.

"No," she replied, pushing open the door. "Just taking it all in."

They slid into a booth near the back, away from the prying eyes and ears that seemed ever-present in their line of work. A harried waitress dropped off two laminated menus before rushing back to the kitchen's siren call. Clara scanned the menu without really seeing it, her mind still parsing the day's events, searching for some detail that might lead them out of the maze of dead ends.

Derek drummed his fingers on the tabletop, breaking her reverie. "You know, after today, I could eat a horse," he said with a half-smile.

"Let's stick to something that can be legally served in this establishment," Clara responded dryly, returning the smile. She opted for a cheeseburger with fries—a classic comfort food that required little thought.

"Same for me," Derek agreed. "And coffee. Lots of coffee."

Their banter was a well-rehearsed dance, one that allowed them to skirt around the edges of the darkness that their job often brought them face to face with. It was a respite, however fleeting, from the weight of unsolved cases and unspoken fears.

It was easy, in moments like these, to forget the gravity of their occupation. To pretend, if only for the duration of a meal, that they were just two friends unwinding after a long day at the office.

As they waited for their order, the diner's atmosphere wrapped around them—a quilt stitched from hushed conversations, the soft clatter of dishes, and the intermittent hiss of steam from the coffee machine. In a life rife with chaos, such normalcy was a rare gift, one that Clara found herself reluctant to relinquish.

"Next time, I get to pick the place, though," she stated, her tone teasing. "Your taste in diners is almost as questionable as your interrogation techniques."

"Deal." Derek grinned, lifting his mug in a silent toast to their partnership—which often teetered on the brink of friendly rivalry—and to the quiet moments that kept them anchored amidst the storm.

But the moment faded quickly.

Clara fiddled with the ceramic edge of her coffee mug, rotating it slowly as if unraveling an invisible thread. The white noise of the diner had settled into a low hum, a din that seemed to underscore the inner tumult she suddenly felt. With a temporary respite from the investigative work on the case, her mind had time to wander back to her call with her mother that morning, and Clara felt a wave of guilt and sadness at the thought of it.

"Hey," Derek said finally, his voice cutting gently through the ambient sounds. He leaned forward, resting his elbows on the checkered tablecloth. "You've been spinning that cup for like five minutes. What's on your mind?"

She sighed, realizing that Derek's perceptiveness could be as much a balm as it was a gentle indictment of her guarded nature. Clara set the mug down, her eyes tracing the squares on the tablecloth before meeting his gaze.

"It's my mother," she started, her words tentative, like footprints left in fresh snow. "She called today." Clara paused, considering how much to divulge, how much of her personal frost to let him thaw.

"Your mother?" Derek prodded lightly, his expression kindling with concern. "That's rare, isn't it? Is everything okay?"

"Far from it," Clara replied, a dry laugh escaping her like steam. "She told me she and my father are getting divorced. They've been separated for over a year, and I—I didn't even know they were having problems. I didn't see it."

Derek took a moment, absorbing the weight of her confession. "Clara, you're one of the best when it comes to noticing the smallest details. But sometimes, the things closest to us are the hardest to see. How are you holding up?"

"Feels like I should have known, you know? Like maybe there were signs that I missed because I was too wrapped up in work or…I don't know. I didn't mean for us to go so long without talking. Like, I wasn't deliberately cutting them out of my life. It just sort of… happened." Her voice trailed off, dissolving into the murmur around them. She looked away, embarrassed by the vulnerability that crept into her words.

"None of this is on you," Derek reassured her, his tone earnest. "Families can be enigmas, even to those inside them. Do you want to talk about it?"

She hesitated, then nodded, grateful for the invitation to unburden herself. "I don't know what to feel, Derek. Anger, relief, sadness—it's all tangled up. And I keep thinking about my brother, wondering if they'd still be together if… you know. Or maybe not even that. Maybe even if we'd just gotten answers. Closure."

"Maybe," Derek conceded, his eyes softening. "Losing a child, it certainly puts a strain on relationships. But there's no point in playing the what-if game, Clara. You can't change the past. All you can do is allow yourself to process the present. Don't rush to untangle those emotions. Let yourself feel them."

The bell above the diner door jangled, momentarily slicing through their exchange. Clara watched a couple enter, laughing in shared secrecy, and felt a pang of longing for such simple intimacy. She turned back to Derek, his presence a steady beacon in the fog that clouded her mind.

"Thanks for listening," she said gratefully. The case at hand, dealing with her parents' divorce, everything always seemed less daunting with Derek beside her. She had always prided herself on her ability to remember, to notice—but perhaps there was solace in sharing the burden of what went unnoticed, too.

"Anytime," Derek replied. "Besides, after Victor Dunn's circus act today, I think we deserved a moment of… normalcy."

"Normal," she echoed, the word feeling foreign on her tongue. Their food arrived, and after they ate and received the check, they rose in tandem, Derek tossing a couple of bills onto the table as Clara shouldered her bag, heavy with case files. The bell above the door signaled their departure, the cold night air sweeping in to replace the warmth they left behind.

The city lay draped in shadows as they walked, streetlights casting puddles of orange on the damp pavement. Clara tugged her coat tighter against the chill, the fabric whispering across her arms like a warning shiver. She turned to Derek, who seemed lost in thought, his breath a cloud of mist that mingled with hers in the frigid air.

"Home and sleep sound good right about now," she said, more to break the silence than anything else.

"Couldn't agree more," he replied, but there was a distant undercurrent to his voice, as if part of him remained locked in the interrogation room with Dunn.

Clara was about to say something else—to make a comment about the importance of hitting the ground running in the morning, but before she could, her phone shattered the stillness, its shrill ringtone slicing through the calm like a scalpel. Both agents froze, knowing what a call at this hour meant. With a sinking feeling, Clara retrieved her phone, the screen an ominous beacon in the dark.

"Agent Pike," she answered, her voice steady despite the adrenaline beginning to course through her veins.

"Clara, it's Shaw," came the director's clipped tone. "I know it's been a long day, but we need you and Agent Morales. Local PD found another girl. Throat slit, just like Jessica Hanley and Cassie Marlowe. It's looking like you were right about this being a serial, and the bodies are starting to pile up."

CHAPTER TWELVE

As she pulled into the parking lot, the headlights of Clara's SUV cut through the darkness, revealing the skeletal remnants of the historic library, now nothing more than charred timbers and crumbling stone reaching out from the earth like the fingers of some long-dead creature. The weight of history pressed down on Clara as she stepped out into the night, the remnants of the once grand structure casting elongated shadows across the ground like dark omens.

Morales followed suit, his brow furrowed in concentration. They moved in tandem toward the crime scene tape fluttering in the evening breeze. The air was heavy with the scent of dampness and decay, a pungent reminder that nature was reclaiming what was once a sanctuary of knowledge and silence.

"Looks like it could collapse any minute," Derek murmured, eyeing the precariously leaning walls.

Ahead of them, bathed in the harsh light of portable floodlights, stood a local cop who seemed to be guarding the entrance to the remains of the library. He was a bulky silhouette against the brightness, shoulders squared, hands clasped in front of him as if bracing against an invisible force.

"Agent Pike, Agent Morales," he greeted, nodding slightly as they approached. His face was weather-beaten, lines carved deeply around his eyes and mouth, suggesting years spent squinting against the sun or perhaps frowning at scenes similar to this one.

"Officer," Clara acknowledged, "we appreciate you securing the scene. What can you tell us?"

"Pretty quiet so far," he said, his voice gruff. "Got the call around eight. Came right over and haven't let anyone in or out except for the coroner's team. They're done with the preliminaries. Vic's name is Naomi Watson."

Clara nodded, a silent thanks for his diligence. He shifted his weight, looking between the two agents, the beam of his flashlight cutting through the darkness as he gestured toward the shadowy interior of the ruins.

"Body's just inside there," he continued, pointing toward an opening that might have been the library's main entrance in another life. "She was lying face up, almost peaceful-like if you didn't know better."

"Any signs of struggle?" Derek asked, his profiler's mind already whirring into action.

"Didn't look like it to me, but I'll let you folks be the judge of that," the officer replied. "I've seen enough to know that looks can be deceiving, especially in cases like these."

"Thank you," Clara said, her eyes already moving past him, drawn inexorably to the gaping maw of the library's entrance. "We'll take it from here."

As they passed the officer, Clara felt the familiar prickle of anticipation at the base of her skull. Every crime scene was a puzzle waiting to be solved, and her mind was already cataloging every scrap of information, every out-of-place stone. But amidst the rush of her analytical process, a cold thread of sorrow wove its way through her thoughts. Another life lost, another family shattered, and somewhere out there, a killer watching and waiting.

Clara stepped over a fallen archway, her boots crunching on the charred remnants of what was once hallowed ground for knowledge. The moonlight was a feeble companion, casting long, haunting shadows across the library's skeleton. Derek trailed behind her, his hand resting on the gun holstered at his side—a subconscious comfort in the face of the unknown.

"Oh, found somethin' you might wanna see," the officer called out, his voice echoing slightly off the stone debris.

He held up an evidence bag, angling it so the dim light caught the surface of a photo within. It was a sepia-toned image of the library in its glory days, tall columns and proud arches untouched by flame or time.

"It was, uh, near the body," he said with a nod, passing the bag to Clara.

Her fingers brushed against the plastic as she took it, the tactile sensation grounding her amidst the turmoil of the scene. The photograph was an anomaly, a piece of history that had no place among the ruins except as a relic of the past—and someone had made it a part of Naomi's final story.

"Any idea why this was left here?" Derek asked, peering over her shoulder at the image.

"None," she replied, her eyes scanning the photo for any clue hidden in its angles and shadows. "But it definitely seems deliberate."

"Could be a message," he suggested.

"Or a signature," Clara countered, her mind racing through the possibilities. "But it's not consistent with our previous scenes."

"Think we're dealing with a copycat?" Derek questioned, skepticism lacing his tone.

"Maybe," Clara murmured, but her gut twisted with doubt. Each piece of evidence was a thread, and this photograph felt like it belonged to a different tapestry.

They moved closer to where Naomi Watson's body lay, the sight of her still form sending a shiver down Clara's spine. Even in death, there was an elegance to Naomi, a grace that seemed incongruous with the violence of her end.

"Look at her hands," Clara pointed out softly, kneeling beside the body.

Derek crouched next to her, his gaze following her gesture. Naomi's hands were folded together as if in repose.

"Same as the others," he noted, his voice low. "But that picture…"

"Doesn't fit," Clara finished for him, her mind a whirlwind of thought. She could remember every detail of the previous crime scenes as if they were etched into her very soul. And nowhere in those memories was there a token like this.

"Could be a red herring," Derek suggested. "To throw us off."

"Or the evolution of the killer's M.O.," Clara pondered aloud. Each victim had been left with a sense of reverence, a care that spoke of a killer with a deep connection to their lives. But the addition of the photograph hinted at something more, a depth of connection to the location itself.

"Let's not get ahead of ourselves," Derek said, a cautionary note in his voice that pulled Clara back from the edge of her thoughts.

"Right," she agreed, taking a deep breath. "One step at a time."

Yet, as she stared at the vintage photo once more, Clara couldn't shake the feeling that they were missing a crucial piece of the puzzle—one that could potentially lead them straight to the killer's door. Still, she knew she needed to heed Derek's advice. It was essential not to let herself get tunnel vision.

Nearby, the local cop, Officer Hendricks, was securing the perimeter, his silhouette a steadfast guardian against the tapestry of destruction.

"Officer Hendricks," Clara called out, her voice slicing through the eerie silence that had settled over the library's remains. "Has anyone looked into whether Naomi had ties to this library?"

He turned, the beam of his flashlight briefly catching on something in the distance before settling on her face.

"We didn't get that far," Hendricks replied, the brim of his hat casting a shadow over his eyes. "Got word early on that the FBI was gonna be taking lead. Figured you'd want to handle all aspects of the investigation."

"Appreciate it," Derek chimed in, his tone suggesting both gratitude and frustration. He shared a glance with Clara, a silent agreement passing between them. This detail could be crucial.

"Thank you, Officer. We'll take it from here," Clara said, offering a nod before turning away.

The wind whispered through the hollowed-out remains of the library, carrying with it the scent of old ash and decay. It was as if the building itself mourned its own loss, a poignant reminder of the fire that once ravaged its contents, consuming knowledge and history in its greedy flames.

As they stepped away from Hendricks, Clara pulled out her smartphone and quickly navigated to the local historical society's digital archives. Her fingers flew across the screen, each tap a drumbeat in the quiet night. Derek leaned in, watching over her shoulder as titles and dates blurred past until one caught her eye—a news article dated back nearly two decades, the headline screaming tragedy in bold letters: "Local Library Engulfed by Flames."

The title alone was enough to trigger Clara's perfect recall. She remembered seeing that article in the paper the day it was published. Instantly, she remembered every detail. The description of the fire. The way the paramedics had come to clear the building and, after thinking they had everyone had gotten out, realized there was a child unaccounted for. She recalled the grainy black-and-white photo accompanying the article of a young girl being pulled from the building just before the ceiling collapsed.

"Look below the eighth paragraph, right-hand side," Clara said, firmly. "There should be a picture."

Derek didn't ask questions; instead, he simply scrolled as Clara told him to. She tapped on the photo, enlarging it, and Derek audibly gasped. There was no mistaking the resemblance.

"Naomi," Derek murmured, his gaze fixed on the screen.

"Her history is entwined with this place," Clara concluded, a chill running down her spine as the pieces fell into place. Naomi Watson, once a little girl who had nearly died in a devastating fire, had returned to the library—only this time, she wouldn't leave alive.

With the revelation hanging between them, Clara pocketed her phone, the weight of the device suddenly feeling like an anchor dragging her deeper into the abyss of this case. The sunken garden where Naomi's body had been found seemed to grow darker, the shadows lengthening as if to obscure the scene from their prying eyes.

"This isn't just about revisiting trauma," Derek mused. "That picture—the killer's taunting us, showing us they know more about the victims than anyone else."

"Or maybe it's a challenge," Clara proposed, her mind racing with possibilities. "A dare for us to unravel their motives." Her eyes caught on a piece of half-burnt wood, which lay like a silent witness to the cruelty that had unfolded among the ruins.

"Either way," Derek added, "we're dealing with someone who's not only aware of the victims' backgrounds but also uses that knowledge to fuel their actions."

"Which means..." Clara's voice trailed off as a cold certainty settled over her. "...there will be more. He won't stop until he's forced to." It was a chilling thought, one that gnawed at her with teeth sharp as the splinters of wood scattered around them.

"Let's get back to the office," Clara finally said, determination etched into her features. "We need to profile these connections, find out what makes these locations so significant to the killer."

"Agreed," Derek replied. "But we should hurry. If we're right, time isn't on our side."

They turned away from the library's skeletal remains, leaving the scene behind but carrying its weight with them. As they walked back to their car, the moon hovered silently above, reminding them that the day was over, but their search for answers—and the killer's game—was far from finished.

CHAPTER THIRTEEN

The fluorescent lights of the corridor flickered, casting a sickly glow over the linoleum floor as Clara Pike strode down the hallway, her footsteps echoing in the empty space. The weight of the day's revelations hung heavily upon her shoulders, the image of Naomi's lifeless body etched into her memory with cruel precision. She couldn't shake it the way Derek could—not when Clara could see the exact blood pattern and the cold, unblinking eyes every time she closed her own eyes.

"Clara." Derek's voice pulled her back from the edge of her thoughts, his hand resting gently on her arm. "We're spinning our wheels here. Forensics will take time to process everything. We need to step back."

She paused, the blood in her veins firing like electric currents at the mention of more waiting. "I can't shake this feeling, Derek," she said, her gaze fixed on the distant shadows cast by the interrogation rooms. "There's something we're not seeing, and every minute we waste…"

"Is a minute we can use to regroup." His words cut through her resistance, calm and resolute. Derek stood firmly, an anchoring presence in the tempest of her mind. "It's past one in the morning, Clara. Our brains aren't wired for this kind of marathon without rest."

Resisting the urge to pace, to let her restless energy carry her back to the heart of their investigation, Clara clenched and unclenched her fists. Her eyes, usually sharp and discerning, were clouded with fatigue. She knew Derek was right; they had exhausted their leads, and the crime scene was now a labyrinth of evidence awaiting forensic dissection.

"Okay," she conceded, her voice a mere whisper against the humming of the overhead lights. "Let's call it a night." The reluctance in her tone betrayed her inner turmoil, but she could not deny the logic in his plea or the heaviness of her own eyelids.

As they exited the building, the night air felt cool against her skin, a stark contrast to the stifling atmosphere inside. Clara allowed herself to be guided toward the car, her steps automatic as if her body recognized the need for rest even if her mind rebelled against it.

"Fresh eyes," Derek murmured almost to himself as he unlocked the vehicle. "Sometimes that's all it takes to see the answer that's been hiding in plain sight."

"Let's hope so," Clara replied, sliding into the passenger seat. As Derek started the engine, the dashboard lights illuminated the weariness etched on both their faces. They shared a look, an unspoken understanding that, despite the stillness of the world around them at this dark hour, the undercurrents of their case continued to churn relentlessly.

In silence, they drove through the deserted streets, each lost in their own thoughts, the city's slumbering façades flashing by like scenes from a forgotten dream. Clara's mind wandered back to the photograph, to the haunting detail of its placement, a silent scream in the quiet aftermath of violence.

"Get some sleep," Derek said as he pulled up outside her apartment building, his voice soft yet firm. "Tomorrow is another day, another chance to catch this killer."

"Thank you, Derek," Clara managed to say, though gratitude mingled with frustration within her. She stepped out of the car, the night wrapping around her like a cold embrace.

As she walked toward her door, the emptiness of the street mirrored the emptiness of her hands—no new leads to cling to, only the promise of a few hours' escape in sleep. Tomorrow, she would return to the fray, her resolve undiminished, her mind ready to unlock the secrets that danced just beyond her grasp. But tonight, surrender was her only recourse, and oblivion her temporary ally.

Clara closed her apartment door behind her with a soft click that echoed louder than she expected in the stillness of her home. The darkness within seemed to swallow her whole, just as the case threatened to do. But with each step toward her bedroom, she peeled away layers of the day—each clue that led nowhere, every dead end that mocked their efforts. Shedding her jacket and holster, she was now simply a woman, not an FBI agent, ready to succumb to the night's mercy.

The sheets were cool against her skin as she slipped between them, the cotton whispering promises of respite. The room was cast in shadow, the only light a sliver of silver moonlight that painted a ghostly stripe across her bed. Her head sank into the pillow, heavy with the weight of unsolved mysteries, and she felt herself slipping, falling into sleep's embrace with an ease that surprised her. It seemed her exhausted body had betrayed her racing mind, demanding the rest she was reluctant to give.

Her world turned black, a canvas wiped clean, but not for long…

Suddenly, there it was again—the house from her childhood, its familiar walls enclosing her in a suffocating grip. She found herself standing in the living room, the faded wallpaper peeling like aged skin, every detail meticulously reconstructed by her photographic memory. This was no sanctuary; it was the stage for her darkest moment, the unresolved symphony of her brother's unsolved murder.

The air was thick, laced with the scent of old grief and stagnant time. She could hear the clock ticking, counting down to something inevitable, something dreadful. The atmosphere was charged with an electric foreboding that raised the hairs on the back of her neck.

"Clara," a voice whispered, and she turned to see her brother standing there, his eyes pools of sorrow and accusation. "All those cases solved, and you still haven't found out what happened to me yet?"

She reached out to him, desperate to bridge the gap between life and death, to pull him back to her, but he was always just out of reach. His figure blurred and distorted, becoming a shadow that danced just beyond the edge of reality. And then the room shifted, walls bleeding into darkness, floor falling away…

With a violent start, Clara awoke, her breath coming in sharp gasps that cut through the silence of her room. She lay there, heart hammering against her ribcage, sweat beading her forehead. The nightmare clung to her like a second skin, its tendrils retreating slowly into the corners of her consciousness.

It was just a dream, she told herself, a cruel trick played by her own mind. Yet she couldn't quite shake the feeling there was something else, too. Something she was supposed to see but was somehow missing.

With the chill of the early morning air nipping at her skin, Clara stood before the bathroom mirror. The harsh overhead light cast unforgiving shadows across her face, accentuating the dark circles that had taken up permanent residence under her eyes. She splashed cold water on her cheeks, watching the droplets ripple out and distort her reflection—a small metaphor for how she felt inside. As she reached for a towel, her mind replayed fragments of the nightmare; it was as though her subconscious was trying to piece together a puzzle with missing parts.

The usual post-nightmare routine did little to shake off the heavy weight that pressed on her chest. Clara methodically brushed her teeth, the bristles scraping rhythmically against enamel, yet her thoughts were elsewhere, fixated on the dream's intangible unease. Her brother's haunting presence lingered like smoke, but there was more—something else that nudged at the edges of her memory, just beyond her grasp.

She dressed swiftly in her standard attire: a tailored shirt paired with slacks, an ensemble that spoke of both professionalism and the readiness to spring into action. But even as she slid her arms through the sleeves of her jacket, her mind continued its relentless churn. What was it about the nightmare that felt so pressing, so urgent?

Clara froze, the motion of putting on her shoes abruptly halted by a flash of insight. There had been something in the dream, a detail so specific that it couldn't be mere fiction conjured by her overwrought mind. A picture. Not just any picture, but one from the crime scene—the vintage photograph of the old historic library where Naomi had drawn her last breath. In the dream, it sat on the mantel of her childhood home, a place it had no right to be.

Her pulse quickened. The photograph in her dream was a haunting echo of reality, its placement among her family's memories jarring and out of context. It didn't belong there, not amidst the collection of mundane moments and smiling faces. The realization sent a shiver down her spine. Could it be a fragment of her photographic memory surfacing in her sleep—trying to tell her something important? Or was it simply the stress of the case weaving itself into the fabric of her dreams?

Clara shook her head, trying to rid herself of the cobwebs of sleep and the remnants of terror. The apartment was silent around her, waiting for the day to begin, but she was already miles ahead, her mind racing toward the implications of this anomalous detail. If her brain was indeed sifting through the evidence while she slept, then perhaps it was onto something—a meaning to the clue that everyone else had overlooked.

Determined now, Clara finished putting on her shoes, her movements brisk and purposeful. She needed to see that photograph again, to scour it for the detail that had infiltrated her dream. It wasn't just a picture—it was a potential key that could unlock the twisted motivations behind the series of deaths that had left a trail of grief in their wake.

Clara's fingers trembled slightly as they traced the edge of her nightstand, reaching for the phone in a motion that was both deliberate and desperate. The image of the photograph from her dream refused to fade, burning in her mind with an intensity that bordered on obsession. It was more than just a picture; it was a siren call, beckoning her toward a truth hidden just beyond reach.

Her apartment, usually a haven of solace, now felt like a cage. The darkness outside her window seemed to press against the glass, thick with unanswered questions and secrets that lurked in the shadows. Every tick of the clock was a reminder of time slipping away, each second a lost opportunity to unravel the mystery that wound its way through her thoughts.

With a sense of urgency propelling her, Clara dialed Derek's number, her ears straining for the sound of his voice amidst the electronic purr of the line connecting. The ring was an echo in the silence, a harbinger of the disruption she was about to cause in the stillness of the predawn hours.

"Hello?" Derek's voice was thick with sleep, a groggy counterpoint to the keen edge of Clara's wakefulness.

"Derek, it's Clara," she said, words rushing out as if afraid they'd be trapped inside her if she didn't speak quickly enough. "I had a dream about the case. About the photograph."

There was a pause, a rustling sound that spoke of Derek sitting up, trying to shake off the remnants of sleep to be present for whatever drove Clara to call him at this ungodly hour.

"Clara, it's four AM. What's going on?"

"I need you to meet me at headquarters. Now," she insisted, her voice not just urgent but commanding, brooking no argument. "Something about that photograph is important, and I think my dream… It's trying to show us something we've missed."

Derek exhaled slowly, a sign of his internal debate, weighing the necessity of rest against the fervor in Clara's plea. She could almost see him rubbing the bridge of his nose, a gesture he made when grappling with the weight of their responsibility against the strain of fatigue.

"Alright, Clara. Give me half an hour."

"Thank you." There was relief in her voice, tempered by the knowledge that every minute counted. As she hung up the phone, the quiet returned, but it was no longer oppressive. It was a canvas waiting to be filled with the strokes of discovery, and Clara was ready to paint.

CHAPTER FOURTEEN

The fluorescent bulbs of the FBI station flickered overhead, casting a sterile glow on the sea of desks cluttered with case files and coffee mugs. Clara stood before the corkboard wall that had become a shrine to their latest case, her gaze locked on the crime scene photo pinned at the center. More specifically, on the vintage photograph that was found next to the latest victim's body, its edges crinkled like dry autumn leaves.

"Damn it," she muttered under her breath. The dream she'd had, the one where her brother's visit was tangled up with the memory of this very photo—it couldn't be a coincidence. Her mind was a vault, but lately, it felt more like a mausoleum, housing ghosts that refused to rest. She could feel Derek's presence behind her, steady and grounding, yet she knew he was waiting for her to make the next move.

"Clara." Derek finally broke the silence, his voice measured. "You're doing it again."

She turned to face him, the chill of the room seeping into her bones. "Doing what?"

"Chasing shadows." He crossed his arms, regarding her with a concern that bordered on frustration. "Look, I know you want this to mean something, but we have to stay rational. We can't afford to go down rabbit holes based on—"

"Based on what?" Clara cut in sharply, her eyes blazing with an intensity that made Derek take a half-step back. "Intuition? Evidence? This photograph was at Naomi's crime scene for a reason, Derek. And I'm not willing to write it off as a fluke."

"It is strange," Derek conceded, his eyes tracing the perimeter of the image. "A sepia-toned snapshot amidst the chaos."

Clara nodded, feeling her pulse level at the sound of Derek's concession, though her stomach churned as her photographic memory redeveloped every gruesome detail of Naomi's murder in her mind's eye. The photograph's presence at the scene niggled persistently at her intuition like a splinter under the skin. In a case where every clue felt as slippery as trying to grasp water, this felt tangible.

"It could be a game-changer," she said, her voice a low hum filled with both hope and trepidation.

Derek leaned against the edge of a desk, arms crossed as he considered the implications. "If our killer is evolving, adding trophies or messages, it's significant. A deviation from their pattern could tell us more about their psyche, maybe even help us predict their next move."

"Or," he continued, his brow furrowing with caution, "it's a red herring. At the risk of making you angry with me, the reality is we don't know for sure it's connected. The victim might've had it on her. Could be a personal item, or maybe she stumbled upon it."

Clara felt her hands clench slightly at the sound of Derek's further hesitation. The thought of discounting a potentially crucial lead due to uncertainty gnawed at her. She wasn't one to let go easily—not with the stakes so high, and especially not when she had the strong feeling her subconscious was trying to tell her something.

"Maybe," Clara offered, her tone laced with skepticism. "But what are the odds? Everything has significance, Derek. You of all people should know that."

Her partner's history—a botched undercover operation that left him wary of overlooked details—made him meticulous, much like herself. They were two sides of the same coin; she was drawn to the minutiae, while he sought the broader narrative they spun.

Derek sighed, running a hand through his hair. It was a gesture that spoke volumes of their shared exhaustion—the weight of unsolved cases pressing down on them like leaden skies before a storm. "Okay," he conceded, his voice softer now. "We'll look into it further."

"Thank you," Clara replied, her voice softening, too. "I know you're not sold on the idea, but I appreciate you trusting me."

"Always," Derek replied. "But don't thank me yet. I'm open to trying to investigate the photo, but I don't actually have any concrete ideas on how we do that."

For a moment, Clara wasn't sure either. Forensics had already dusted the picture for prints, but there were none. They knew what location was featured in the picture, so there was nothing to research there either.

And then it hit her.

"Reverse image search," she suggested abruptly, her mind snapping together pieces of a puzzle only she could see. "We use the photo, run it through databases, the internet. See if it pops up anywhere else—anywhere that might give us context."

Derek considered Clara's proposal, and for a moment, there was a flicker of admiration in his eyes. "That's not a bad idea," he admitted.

"It could give us a lead on where the picture came from, maybe even tie it to other scenes if this is part of the killer's signature."

"Exactly," Clara said, feeling a surge of determination. The digital tendrils of the internet would serve as their net, and they were going to trawl its depths for any scrap of information that could lead them closer to understanding the mind behind the madness.

"Alright." Derek nodded, pulling out his phone and starting to tap away at the screen. "Let's run the search. But you take lead on examining the results. You're the one with the eye for details. If there's anything out there connected to this photo, you'll find it."

As Derek set about doing the grunt work, Clara's gaze returned to the photograph. The notion that this small piece of paper could be the key to unlocking a murderer's mind sent a shiver down her spine.

"Here," Derek said, handing her his phone. "See what you can find."

Clara scrolled through the results with a speed that matched her racing heart. The screen's glow cast an ethereal light on her concentrated face as images cascaded down, the result of the reverse image search Derek had initiated. Little by little, the digital puzzle pieces began to align until one photograph halted her frantic scrolling—a sepia-toned image of an old iron bridge, hauntingly similar to the photograph from Naomi's crime scene.

"This might be something," Clara said, voice laced with a controlled urgency that demanded attention.

Derek leaned over her shoulder, his eyes narrowing as he scrutinized the screen.

"There's definitely a similar style," Derek agreed. "But there's not enough here to tell us much."

"Eh—give me time," Clara replied. "We haven't even checked the metadata yet."

Her comment about the metadata proved to be prescient, as investigating the metadata attached to the image led them to a collection—a series of vintage landmark photographs. Clara's pulse quickened as she clicked through a virtual gallery showcasing architectural relics caught in time. But it was the name associated with the collection that ensnared her focus: Oliver Belmont, a local art dealer with a penchant for the past.

"Oliver Belmont," Derek repeated, reading over her shoulder. "Why does that name sound familiar?"

"Because he's been on the periphery of two other cases this year," Clara replied, reports from the two other cases immediately populating in her mind's eye. She could still see the slight smudge beside Oliver's name on the first report where the detective's hand had blurred the wet ink. "Invitations to his gallery openings were found in the victims' mail."

"Coincidence?" Derek mused, skeptical.

"Too many coincidences make a pattern," Clara countered, her mind weaving connections. The notion that this man could be more than just a purveyor of fine art chilled her. If the photograph was indeed a part of Belmont's collection, it might mean the killer had a direct link to him—or perhaps, was Belmont himself.

"According to this," Clara pointed at the screen, where the details of the gallery were listed, "the collection is on display at Belmont's gallery downtown."

"Time for a field trip then," Derek said, grabbing his coat from the back of his chair. "Let's go see these photographs up close and have a chat with Mr. Belmont."

Clara nodded, saving the webpage onto a flash drive and slipping her own jacket on. The gallery wasn't far, but as they stepped out into the brisk air, the short distance felt like a journey into the unknown. Every step toward the address seemed to echo with the weight of the unsolved mystery that loomed over them.

The city unfurled around them as they walked, a concrete maze under a sky heavy with unshed rain. Each building, each alleyway, whispered secrets of its own—secrets that hovered just beyond reach. Clara felt the tendrils of her nightmare intertwine with reality, the grainy image from her sleep merging with the tangible world.

They reached the gallery situated in an older part of town. Its exterior was nondescript, easily missed if not for the subtle sign bearing Belmont's name. The large front window offered a peek inside, a curated world of refined taste and hushed tones.

"Ready?" Derek asked, his hand resting on the door handle.

"Let's do this," Clara affirmed, steeling herself for whatever lay within.

As the door opened, a bell chimed softly above them, announcing their arrival to anyone who might be listening. Clara stepped over the threshold of Belmont Gallery with a sense of foreboding that seemed to cling to her like a second skin. The quiet of the space was almost reverential, and it wrapped around them, muting their footsteps on the polished concrete floor. Derek was close behind, his presence a steadying force amid the uncertainty that fluttered in her chest.

"Oliver Belmont?" Clara called out, her voice threading through the room's stillness. No answer came; only their echoes returned as if the gallery itself were holding its breath.

"Doesn't seem like he's here," Derek observed, his eyes scanning the expanse of the room. "Might as well take a look around."

Clara nodded, and they parted ways, each drawn to different sections of the immaculately curated space. She moved between the displays, her gaze flitting from canvas to frame, searching for something, anything, that might lead them to understanding the photograph from Naomi's crime scene.

The gallery was a shrine to moments frozen in time, each piece a fragment of history that whispered secrets of eras long past. Yet none spoke louder than the collection nestled in the back corner, a congregation of monochrome prints that beckoned her closer. Her heart thrummed a frantic rhythm as she approached, the air thickening with each step.

There, amidst the still lifes and landscapes, hung a series of vintage photographs, each depicting landmarks with an eerie familiarity. They were kin to the image found beside Naomi's lifeless form, echoes of the same haunting aesthetic. Clara's fingertips grazed the brass plaque beneath one particular photo, and she caught her breath. It was unmistakable—the auditorium where Cassie Marlowe had met her untimely end, captured in greyscale solemnity.

"Look at this," Clara murmured, barely audible yet loud enough for Derek, who'd circled back to her side. His eyes followed her gesture, widening slightly as recognition dawned.

"Same style, same vintage feel," he said, his voice low but laced with urgency. "That plus the fact that it's of another one of our crime scenes. You know what they say. Twice is a coincidence, but—"

"Three things is a pattern," Clara finished for him, her mind racing. "He has a photo of Cassie's murder site. This is our link, Derek. This has to be."

The pieces of the puzzle were aligning, each revelation another brushstroke on a canvas of malice and intent. Clara felt the weight of the discovery settle upon her shoulders, a grim mantle that both propelled and haunted her pursuit of the truth. As she stood there, enveloped by the shadows of the gallery and the ghosts of the images on display, the ominous undercurrent of the investigation pulsed ever stronger.

CHAPTER FIFTEEN

The early morning sun cast long shadows across the parquet floor of the gallery, wrapping Clara and Derek in a cloak of eerie half-light. The air was thick with the musky fragrance of aging paper and polished wood, a scent that usually comforted Clara but now only heightened her tension. As her gaze lingered on the photograph—a monochrome snapshot of the auditorium that was identical to the first crime scene—her pulse quickened.

"Oliver Belmont," Clara murmured, tapping the glass that shielded the photo. "He's our guy, Derek. This can't be a coincidence."

To her surprise, rather than joining her in her enthusiasm, Derek simply sighed.

"What?" Clara snapped. "What's your problem?"

"Nothing," he said, his tone borderline sullen.

"Look, I know sometimes you think I can get ahead of myself, especially when it comes to visual evidence, but look at it!" she insisted, pointing to the photograph with an almost feverish intensity. "The angle, the lighting—it's too exact. And the fact that it's of Cassie Marlow's murder site? It's beyond coincidental."

Derek leaned in closer, his dark eyes reflecting the vintage image. "This gallery is public. Anyone could have snapped a picture of this and left it for us to find."

"Or maybe," Clara countered, "it's a signature. Oliver Belmont deals in these images daily. He knows them, he has access to them, and now one shows up at a murder scene? We can't ignore that."

Derek ran a hand through his hair, his brow furrowed in thought. "I hear you, but without solid evidence, Belmont is just another art dealer."

"Then let's go talk to him," Clara proposed, her jaw set in determination. "If he's innocent, he'll have nothing to hide."

"Alright," Derek conceded, albeit reluctantly. "Let's find Belmont and see what he has to say for himself."

Clara nodded, her mind already racing ahead, cataloging every detail from the photograph that they might use in their questioning.

Clara's stride was long and purposeful as they began circling the gallery, searching, if not for Oliver Belmont, then at least for someone who worked there and might be able to identify his whereabouts.

"Clara, you need to pace yourself," Derek said, keeping up with her brisk walk. "Even if Belmont is involved, confronting him without solid proof could spook him, or worse—compromise the investigation."

"Then we'll be careful," Clara replied. "We ask questions, we observe. That's what we do."

"Okay, I'm just saying that just because your memory is perfect doesn't mean you're always right," Derek remarked, casting a sidelong glance at her. "We're not even sure this guy knows part of his collection was used at a crime scene."

"Which is why we need to find out," Clara pressed. "If there's a chance he's connected, we owe it to the victims to pursue it."

Derek exhaled slowly, measuring his next words with care. "I know that. You know I know that. That's why we're here. But not everything is a clue, Clara. Sometimes a photograph is just a photograph."

"Sometimes," she agreed absently, her focus unwavering. "But sometimes, it's the key to unlocking everything. You taught me to trust my gut, Derek. My gut says this lead is real."

"Okay," Derek relented, a hint of admiration in his voice at her tenacity. "We'll follow your lead on this one, but we do it by the book. Belmont deserves the presumption of innocence until proven guilty."

"Agreed," Clara acknowledged, feeling the familiar surge of resolve within her. She would not let impatience cloud her judgment, not with so much at stake.

"Can I help you?" A young attendant approached, her voice slicing through the quiet ambience. She wore a crisp white blouse paired with black slacks, a silver name tag pinned just above her heart: "Sophie."

"I'm Special Agent Clara Pike with the FBI," Clara introduced herself, presenting her badge subtly as to not draw attention from the sparse patrons lingering in contemplation before the artworks. "This is my partner, Special Agent Derek Morales. We're looking for Mr. Belmont."

"Oliver is away at a meeting right now with a local artist," Sophie informed them, her tone professional yet tinged with an apologetic note. "He's quite strict about not being disturbed."

"Could we get the name of the artist he's meeting with?" Derek interjected smoothly, his posture relaxed but eyes keenly observant.

"Of course, Agent Morales." Sophie glanced at a schedule on her tablet. "It's with Emilia Voss. She's discussing a new exhibition."

"Where can we find Ms. Voss's studio?" Clara asked, her mind already mapping out their next move.

"Just down the street, 145 Halcyon Avenue," Sophie replied, pointing toward the large front windows. "You can't miss it. The building has a large mural of a phoenix on the side. She's in studio 3B, but, as I said, he really doesn't like to be disturbed. If at all possible, it really would be preferable if you—"

"Thank you, Sophie," Clara interrupted, offering a polite nod before turning toward the exit. When a killer was on the loose, waiting simply wasn't an option.

Stepping back onto the sidewalk, Derek and Clara found themselves enveloped by the early-morning murmur and bustle of the city. Buildings stretched toward the sky like silent giants, their windows reflecting the gray clouds overhead, giving the day an oppressive weight.

"Right down the street, huh?" Derek commented, glancing at the address scribbled in his notebook.

"Well, that's the first break we've had all day," Clara replied. Her thoughts swirled with the possibilities this lead could unravel, and even right down the street was farther than she wanted to travel. She didn't want to wait one moment longer for answers than she had to. She would have teleported to Emilia Voss's studio if she could.

The walk to the artist's studio was short, but every step seemed deliberate, heavy with expectation. Clara observed the passersby, wondering if any had unwittingly brushed shoulders with a killer. The air hung heavy with an unspoken menace, a sense that unseen eyes might be watching from the shadows cast by overhanging balconies and fire escapes.

As they arrived at 145 Halcyon Avenue, the promised mural loomed before them—a vivid splash of oranges and reds against the drab backdrop of the city. The phoenix spread its wings wide, flames licking its feathers as it rose from ashes, depicted in painstaking detail at the base of the wall.

"Quite the landmark," Derek muttered, taking in the artwork.

"Let's just hope it's a good omen," Clara replied, her hand resting on the grip of her service weapon—a habit when the air smelled like trouble.

The door to the building was unlocked, so, without another word, they entered, the door creaking on its hinges—ominous, like the first note of a suspenseful symphony. Inside, the scent of oil paint and turpentine greeted them, a stark contrast to the sterile chill of the gallery they'd just left. The hallway was narrow, claustrophobic, with doors lining either side like silent sentries guarding the secrets within.

"Studio 3B," Clara noted, spotting the gold-plated numbers affixed to a door halfway down the corridor.

Derek gave her a curt nod, and together, they approached. Clara could feel the thrum of her pulse in her fingertips, the anticipation of what might lie beyond this threshold. With each case, there was always a moment before the reveal, where the truth was just out of reach but coming ever closer, and she lived for it.

Raising her hand, she knocked firmly on the door marked 3B, ready to face whatever was on the other side.

The door swung open with a languid ease, revealing Emilia Voss, a stunning artist in her early fifties with wild hair and bright eyes.

"May I help you?" she asked, surprised to see them.

"Yes, thank you," Clara began. "I'm Special Agent Pike, and this is my partner, Special Agent Morales. We're with the FBI."

"Pleasure to meet you," Derek added.

"You, too," Emilia replied. "What can I do for you?"

"We're here to speak with Oliver Belmont," Clara said.

"Interesting," Emilia responded before turning to face the interior of her studio.

"Ollie!" she called, and something in Clara's gut told her Emilia Voss was probably the only person who could get away with calling him that.

A moment later, Oliver Belmont appeared. He stood framed by the chaos of his artist's sanctuary, every inch the epitome of arrogance with a posture that managed to look down on them from his average height. His eyes, sharp and assessing, flickered over Clara's badge before meeting her unwavering gaze.

"They're from the FBI," Emilia told him. "Agents Pike and Morales, right?"

"Yes," Derek affirmed.

"They came to speak with you," Emilia added before walking over to an easel and picking up her brush.

"How thrilling," Oliver replied, turning his attention from Emilia to the agents standing before him. "What could you possibly want with little old me?"

"Mr. Belmont," Clara began, her tone even, betraying none of the irritation that prickled beneath her skin, "There was a photo found at a recent crime scene that is very similar to the pieces in a collection from your gallery. We were hoping to speak with you about it."

"Interesting. My art does tend to evoke strong emotions," Oliver mused, leaning against the doorjamb as if he had all the time in the world. "But I'm quite certain it hasn't killed anyone."

"Maybe not," Derek interjected, stepping forward, "but we believe you can help us understand why it was there. So we'd like to speak with you. Down at headquarters if possible."

Oliver sighed theatrically, glancing back into the studio as though considering whether they were worthy of his time. Clara noticed the subtle shift in his shoulders—a sign of annoyance or perhaps something more. Her mind cataloged the tension in his jaw, the fleeting shadows across his expression.

"Fine," Oliver relented after a beat too long, straightening up. "Let's get this over with."

As they escorted him out, Clara couldn't shake the feeling that Oliver's acquiescence was a performance, another layer in a facade meant to throw them off his scent.

***

The interrogation room at headquarters was sterile and uninviting, a stark contrast to the vibrant disorder of Emilia Voss's studio. The one-way glass reflected their images back at them, giving the illusion of a crowded space when, in reality, it was just Clara, Derek, and their suspect.

Oliver sat across from them, his body language casual to the point of insolence, fingers drumming an idle rhythm on the metal table.

"Let's talk about Cassie Marlowe," Clara began, her tone deliberate, knowing full well the weight each word carried in the confined space. "A photograph of the building where she was murdered was found at your gallery."

"There are lots of photographs of buildings at my gallery, Miss Pike," Oliver replied, his use of "Miss" designed, quite clearly, to get under Clara's skin.

"And I can assure you, I don't know any Clara Marlowe," he added.

"Cassie Marlowe," Clara corrected.

"Whatever," he replied with a shrug. Clara sighed. She was finding it nearly impossible not to let Oliver's shtick get under her skin.

"Perhaps this will jog your memory," Derek said, sliding a photo of Cassie across the table toward Oliver.

"Pretty," Oliver commented as he eyed Cassie's photograph, but his eyes remained cold, unyielding. "Tragic, what happened to her. But tragic is also mundane these days, isn't it?"

Clara leaned in slightly, her gaze never leaving his. "We're not interested in philosophy, Mr. Belmont. We're interested in facts."

"Of course," Oliver replied with a mock bow of his head. "But as you can see, I am here, not running away, not resisting. Doesn't that tell you something?"

Every answer he gave, every nonchalant shrug, only served to deepen Clara's annoyance. Clara's mind worked overtime, piecing together the enigma of Oliver Belmont, wondering if behind that smug veneer lay the mind of a killer or simply a man too accustomed to being the smartest one in the room. Whatever the case, they'd been at it for half an hour now, and so far, the man had offered them absolutely nothing of use.

"Let's talk alibis then," Derek interjected. "Where were you on the nights in question?"

"I was at the gallery. We've had a big show this week. Lots of parties, celebrations. I was quite the social butterfly at these events, so there will be numerous people who can verify my whereabouts. But, if that's still not enough for you, you can check the CCTV footage. I have to imagine even you wouldn't try to argue with time-stamped video evidence."

"How convenient," Clara said dryly. Her mind raced through possibilities. She had been so sure this photograph meant something. Was it really just a red herring meant to throw them off the true killer's scent? Or could Oliver have tampered with the footage? Hired someone to stand in for him?

"Convenience has nothing to do with it," Oliver shot back, tilting his head slightly. "But efficiency, now that's something I strive for."

"We'll need to verify that, of course," Derek began. "Check the footage, as you suggested. But if that all pans out—"

"Then I'm free to go," Oliver interrupted.

"Yes," Clara said, working hard not to grit her teeth. Oliver certainly wasn't the worst suspect she'd ever interrogated, but she nevertheless found him deeply grating. "You'd be free to go."

"You do that then," Oliver replied, his tone smooth as silk. "And do let me know if there's anything else I can provide to ease your investigative burden."

Clara could feel the swell of a headache as they concluded the interview, and she made her way back to her office. She slumped into her chair, the photograph that had led them to Oliver Belmont lying discarded on her desk. She stared at it, trying to will it to reveal its secrets, to give her something—anything—that would break the case wide open. But the glossy surface offered no answers, only the reflection of a woman grappling with the specter of failure.

"Damn it," she whispered to herself, her hands clenching into fists on the desktop.

Her mind, usually so adept at piecing together fragments of information, felt as foggy as the city streets on a winter morning. She had been so sure that the photograph was a crucial piece of the puzzle, a window into the killer's world. Yet now, all it seemed to do was mock her with its silence.

"Clara, we'll find another way," Derek said, leaning against the doorframe. He watched her with concern etched into his features, knowing all too well the personal toll this case was taking on her.

She shook her head, the weight of unsolved cases pressing down upon her. "We're running out of time, Derek. Another body could turn up any minute, and we're no closer to catching this guy than we were when we started."

"We've cracked tougher cases than this before. We'll do it again," Derek offered, trying to reassure her, though his own doubt was a shadow in his eyes.

"Have we?" Clara stood up abruptly, her gaze returning to the photo. "I thought I saw something in this, a detail everyone else missed. But what good is a photographic memory if all it captures are dead ends?"

"Your gift has helped more than you know," Derek said softly. "This is just a setback. We regroup, we dig deeper."

Clara nodded, though the fire that usually drove her felt like it was dwindling to embers. She appreciated Derek's confidence that they would regroup, dig deeper. But in this exact moment, she had absolutely no idea how.

CHAPTER SIXTEEN

The sterile light of the computer screen bathed the room in an eerie glow as the killer sat hunched over his desk. The soft murmur of Lila Torres's voice filtered through the speakers, a private symphony for his twisted intent. He sipped slowly from a cup of black coffee, the bitter liquid grounding him in the reality of his plan. His fingers danced across the keyboard, pausing the recording at intervals to savor certain confessions, specific vulnerabilities that Lila had offered up to her therapist like sacrificial lambs.

"Nobody really understands." Lila's recorded voice cracked with emotion. "The pressure, the expectation... and when it all came crashing down..."

He let the words hang in the air before hitting play again, letting them mix with the scent of disinfectant that clung to every surface of his meticulously kept home. Around him, the walls were lined with bookshelves, each volume organized by subject and author, a testament to his need for order amidst the chaos he wrought.

His kill kit lay open on the table, a black duffel bag that contained the tools of his grim trade. He'd placed each item within carefully: gloves, cleaning supplies, and a digital camera to capture the moment of reckoning. He also brought with him a vintage photograph of the scene—one he would replace with the new image he would take after his mission had been completed. It was a tangible thing, a physical way of showing the transformation he had completed, both in the women and in the locations that had caused them so much pain.

Each object was a piece of the puzzle, a step in the dance he was about to perform. It was a routine he had perfected three times over, tweaking and developing it each time. Last time, he'd tried leaving the vintage photograph behind instead of destroying it on his return. That felt better. Right. Like he was leaving both the victim and the building's past behind as they forged something new together. He wondered what new discovery he might make today—what new tweak to his plan might heighten the release. The pleasure.

As Lila's voice trembled through another admission of her deepest fears, he reached for the knife. It was his favored instrument—a sleek blade, honed to a deadly edge, with a handle that fit comfortably in his palm as if they were molded together. A cloth lay next to it, and he picked it up, the fabric whispering against the metal as he wiped the blade down. With each stroke, he contemplated his approach, imagining the surprise in Lila's eyes when she realized what was happening.

"Control," she said in the recording, a word that echoed his own sentiments. Yes, control was everything.

As a child, he'd had no control. His father had been more monster than man, the only predictable thing about him his unpredictability and violence. But his mother had been worse. She had been a coward, too afraid to confront the reality of the man she married to do anything about it. She had wasted her whole life trapped in an endless cycle of trauma, too busy living in her own misery to forge her own life.

If that had been all it was, perhaps he could have forgiven her, but it wasn't. She was so wrapped up in her own pain that she couldn't see his. She was his mother, the woman who was supposed to love and protect him unconditionally. But instead, she just stood idly by, nursing her own wounds without any regard for the wounds being inflicted upon him.

If only she'd had someone like him—someone who could force her to truly face her trauma and then punish her for the life she wasted in her blindness. But she hadn't, so their suffering was allowed to simply continue unabated.

But these women wouldn't end up like that. Not now. Not on his watch.

The knife gleamed under the room's fluorescent lights, a beacon of the power he held over life and death.

"Perfect," he whispered to himself, placing the immaculate knife into the duffel. The plan took shape in his mind—precise and calculated. Lila's routine was known to him, her habits studied with obsessive detail. And as he visualized each step, from the silent entry to the swift execution, a shiver of anticipation ran down his spine. The pieces were falling into place, and soon.

The sun perched high in a cloudless sky, its rays unimpeded as they cast long, stark shadows across the pavement. The killer stood by the window, the light casting a harsh glare on his kill kit. Daylight was an unfamiliar accomplice, one that offered no sanctuary of shadows, no veil of darkness to cloak his deeds. He felt the weight of the challenge; this kill demanded more from him—precision.

He reached for the duffel bag, feeling the familiar heft of it in his hand. As he zipped the bag closed, his heartbeat quickened with the thrill of what was to come. This daylight operation was a deviation from his norm, but it heightened the stakes, sharpened his senses. Much like leaving the photograph at the last crime scene, he wondered if perhaps this change, too, would only serve to heighten the experience.

The killer locked his door behind him and descended the steps to the parking lot where his nondescript sedan waited. It was a vehicle chosen for anonymity, its blandness a shield in the urban landscape. He slid into the driver's seat, the leather cool against his skin. With a practiced motion, he inserted the key into the ignition, the engine coming to life with a quiet purr—a contrast to the cacophony of thoughts racing through his mind.

As he navigated the streets toward Lila's gym, the city buzzed around him, alive with the thrum of midday activity. People walked with purpose, their minds occupied with the minutiae of their lives, unaware of the predator in their midst. He drove with deliberate care, obeying traffic laws, blending in. Each turn brought him closer to his destination, to Lila.

The gym loomed ahead, a modern fortress of glass and steel. It was a place where aspirations were built and sometimes shattered—a fitting stage for Lila's final performance. He maneuvered into a parking spot with a clear view of the entrance, the engine going silent as he turned off the car. The gym's facade reflected the world back upon itself, distorted and fragmented. It was a mirror to the chaos he was about to unleash within its walls.

Sitting there, he allowed himself a moment to observe the rhythm of the place, the comings and goings of its patrons. They were all part of the dance, unwitting extras in the scene he was set to direct. His hands rested on the steering wheel, the leather cool and smooth beneath his palms. Soon, they would be warm, alive with the pulse of action, the execution of his plan.

With every passing second, the anticipation built within him like a symphony reaching its crescendo. This was the precipice upon which he teetered—the ultimate balance between risk and reward.

The sunlight was unforgiving in its scrutiny, and he found that made him feel anxious. His fingers tapped an impatient rhythm on the steering wheel, betraying his longing for the shadowy veil of night. In the darkness, his actions were cloaked, his intentions obscured. But the brightness of day laid everything bare, exposing the contours of risk with stark clarity.

"Evening would be better," he murmured to himself, the words a clandestine prayer dissipating into the car's confined space. While he had tried to be optimistic about the thrill that killing in daylight might bring, he realized now that the night had always been his ally, shielding his movements in its comforting embrace. Yet there was no twilight to enshroud him now, no dusk to whisper secrets of silence and stealth. He could almost feel the weight of the sun's gaze upon him, a celestial spotlight that threatened to unveil his darkest intentions.

With a sigh, he steeled himself against the daylight's scrutiny, his resolve hardening like cooled lava. This kill required precision, a choreography that left no room for improvisation. Every step, every breath, had to be measured. The daylight kill was the ultimate test of his mastery, but, as he quickly reminded himself, it was a challenge he was determined to meet head-on.

Settling deeper into the driver's seat, he allowed his gaze to drift across the parking lot toward the large windows of the gym. Through the reflections of cars and clouds, he caught glimpses of Lila at work. Her movements were fluid, her body the epitome of power and grace—a testament to a life dedicated to physical excellence. She was a living sculpture, chiseled from determination and resilience.

But it wasn't admiration that simmered beneath his watchful eyes; it was a cold, calculating intent. He studied her interactions, the way she commanded attention without demanding it, the respect she garnered without a word. It was all part of the image, the facade that needed to be shattered. In his mind, the plan unfolded with each passing moment, a sinister ballet performed in broad daylight.

His hand ventured to the passenger seat, fingers brushing over the canvas bag that lay there. Inside, tools of destruction lay dormant, waiting to be awakened by his touch. They were instruments that would soon sing a song of finality, their metallic chorus a harbinger of Lila's end. It was almost time to begin the performance, and the killer knew his role by heart.

His breath fogged up the glass momentarily, obscuring the vision of the gym within. He wiped it away with a sleeve, his movements mechanical, detached. Inside, Lila continued her work, blissfully unaware of the fate that awaited her. And he, the harbinger of that fate, solidified his intent with each passing second.

"Today, you confront your past," he whispered, more to himself than anyone else. "Today, it ends." Darkness clung to his words, a promise of the suffering he was about to end—or perhaps, the suffering he was destined to continue.

CHAPTER SEVENTEEN

FBI headquarters was a hive of frenzied energy, the fluorescent lights above casting an unforgiving glow on agents bustling between rows of gray cubicles. Clara maneuvered across the room like a ghost, her gaze fixed and unwavering, the undercurrents of chaos around her barely registering as she made her way to her desk. The relentless tick of the clock echoed in her ears, each second slipping away feeling like a personal affront—a reminder of the killer who remained at large.

The photograph from Naomi's crime scene lay before her, its edges frayed from being handled too many times. It depicted a seemingly innocuous library, but Clara's instincts screamed that it held the key they were missing.

"Clara." Derek's voice cut through her concentration, laden with a weariness that mirrored the dark circles under his eyes. "We've been down this road. It's just a picture. There's nothing left for us to learn from it."

She frowned, turning to face him. Derek stood, arms crossed, a pillar of skepticism amidst the clutter of case files and coffee cups that adorned their shared workspace. His doubt was understandable, yet for Clara, it was like a barrier she needed to dismantle, brick by brick.

"If there was nothing left for us to learn from it, then we'd know why it was at the crime scene," she insisted, her tone sharpening with conviction. "There's a pattern here we're not seeing. This photo is a deliberate placement, a piece of the puzzle we can't afford to dismiss."

Derek sighed, running a hand through his hair in a gesture of exasperation. He respected Clara—her keen eye for detail was unmatched—but at times her fixation could be overwhelming. He watched as she leaned forward, elbows resting on the desk, her fingers tracing the outline of the photograph as if willing it to divulge its secrets.

"Look, I get it. You want this to mean something," he said, trying to bridge the gap between his pragmatism and her intuition. "But we have to consider the possibility that we're reaching. Oliver's alibi checks out, so where does that leave us with this?"

The air between them thickened with tension, the weight of unsolved questions pressing down like a physical force.

"Dead ends are just the start of a different path, Derek," she replied, her voice a low murmur of determination. "We can't afford to disregard any lead, no matter how small."

Her partner regarded her for a moment, his expression unreadable. Then, with a resigned nod, he turned back to his own work, leaving Clara to her contemplation. She refocused on the photograph, its significance a gnawing certainty in her gut. There was something there, hidden in plain sight, and she would find it—no matter the skepticism that surrounded her.

She hovered over the glossy surface of the photograph, her eyes narrowed in concentration. The room hummed with the low murmur of agents immersed in their work, but to Clara, it was as if she and Derek were encased in a silent bubble—a pocket of urgency amidst routine diligence. She lifted the photo closer, studying the edges, the way the light played off its vintage finish.

"Consider for a moment," Clara started, her words slicing through the quiet tension, "that our killer is cunning. He leaves this photograph behind not by mistake, but as a deliberate red herring." Her finger hovered above the image of the library back in its glory days. "To lead us to suspect him—Oliver—and while we chase ghosts, the real predator stays one step ahead."

Derek leaned back in his chair, arms crossed over his chest. His brow furrowed, skepticism written across his features like a code Clara couldn't decipher. "So, you're saying this entire thing is a setup? To frame an innocent man?" There was a disbelieving tilt to his voice, one that made Clara's pulse quicken with both irritation and a need to prove her point.

"Exactly. It's misdirection. And given the meticulous nature of these crimes, I wouldn't put it past our killer to use every tool at his disposal, including psychological manipulation," Clara insisted, her voice firm.

The fluorescent lights overhead flickered momentarily, casting shadows that danced across the sterile walls of the FBI headquarters. Rows of desks, laden with case files and computers, bore witness to countless hours of pursuit—each lead a promise, each dead end a disappointment.

Derek shifted, his chair creaking under the movement. "Clara, if that was the plan, why wait until now? Why not plant evidence like this right from the beginning?" Frustration edged his words, his profiler's mind grappling with the logic.

"Because," Clara replied, locking eyes with him, "it's about timing. It's about sowing doubt when we least expect it, throwing us into chaos." She let out a sigh, feeling the weight of the unsolved puzzle pressing down on her.

"Even if you're right," he countered, tapping a pen against the desk, "knowing the photograph is part of some elaborate scheme doesn't get us any closer to a suspect. We're still in the dark, Clara."

"Perhaps," she conceded, the chill of uncertainty threading through her. "But understanding the 'why' behind the 'what' could be the key to unlocking his identity. And I refuse to ignore any piece of this twisted puzzle."

The clock on the wall ticked, a somber reminder that time was slipping away from them, just as the killer remained elusive, hidden amongst shadows and subterfuge. Clara's mind raced, the gears turning as pieces of the mystery began to align in her head—each detail a breadcrumb leading toward an unseen conclusion.

"For heaven's sake, Clara, I'm not ignoring it. I got up in the middle of the night, on two hours of sleep, to discuss it with you. I came in at four in the morning to investigate it with you. I ran a search with you, I went to the gallery with you, I even interrogated a man with you for no reason other than the fact that he had photos that looked like that photo in his art gallery." As he spoke, Clara could see Derek getting angrier and angrier. He rarely lost his temper with her, but she had clearly struck a nerve.

"I have been an extremely supportive partner on this," he continued, that vein in his neck starting to pulse the way it did when he was really, really angry. "And I am trying to be patient because I know you're dealing with a lot right now, but you don't get to accuse me of ignoring you. That's not fair."

Clara knew, instinctively, that she should apologize. Everything Derek was saying was true. He had done all of those things. But she was sleep-deprived and there was a killer on the loose, and she was too hurt, too frustrated by his anger with her to be the bigger person here. So, instead, she just stared at him.

"I'm going home, and I'm going to get some sleep," Derek said, his tone even despite his clenched teeth. "If you have any sense, you will too. We can regroup tomorrow, and concentrate—separately—on individuals who have connections to multiple crime scenes."

With that, he stormed off, leaving a stunned Clara alone behind him.

***

When Clara came back to FBI headquarters a few hours later, sheepish and slightly better rested, she was stunned to find Derek already there, eyes fixed on the computer.

Hearing her footsteps behind him, he turned to her, smiling broadly.

"Check it out," he began. "I think I've got a lead."

And just like that, everything was right between them again—a fact Clara was every bit as grateful for as the promise of a lead.

She crossed to Derek and peered over his shoulder, eyebrows knitting together as she scanned the contents of his screen. Katherine Merrick—event planner extraordinaire, with her elegant handwriting and precise lists. Clara's eyes widened as she read about the gala on the promenade, the charity auction at the school.

"Two crime scenes…" she murmured, her brain piecing together the implications.

"Exactly," Derek confirmed, leaning against the desk. "She organized events at two of the crime scenes. Not only that, but she would have had detailed knowledge of the layouts, the schedules, even the security details. I know there's nothing to connect her to the library yet, but given the state of it…"

It was a solid lead—or, at the very least, a place to look—and Clara felt a begrudging respect for Derek's investigative instincts. It was maddening—he had been right to push for this line of inquiry, and yet she couldn't let go of the photograph, the sense that they were still missing something crucial.

"Yeah, her connection to that one could have been personal. Maybe back from her childhood like it was with Naomi. But either way, the fact that she had intimate knowledge of the first two scenes, it's potentially something," she conceded with a nod. "This Merrick woman… she's worth a closer look."

"Agreed," Derek said. He straightened, a flicker of optimism crossing his features. "I'll start digging into her background, see what connections she might have to our victims."

"Good," Clara replied, closing the file with a snap. Together, they had found a new thread to pull, a hope in the darkness. And yet, as she turned back to her screen, the photograph awaited, its enigma undiminished. There was more here; she was sure of it. But for now, she had no choice but to let Katherine Merrick take center stage in their grim ballet with a killer.

CHAPTER EIGHTEEN

The phone rang with an almost sinister monotony before it was interrupted by the click of a connection. Clara Pike held her cell phone to her ear, feeling the weight of the device as though it were a lifeline to their next lead. The assistant's voice on the other end seemed cheerily oblivious to the macabre dance of death and deduction that had ensnared Clara's every waking moment.

"Katherine Merrick's Events and Design, this is Heidi speaking, how may I assist you today?" came the polished response.

"Hi, Heidi. This is Special Agent Clara Pike. I'm with the FBI, and I need to speak with Katherine Merrick," Clara stated, her voice a blend of professionalism and subtle urgency.

There was a pregnant pause on the line, followed by the crisp tapping of computer keys. "I'm afraid Ms. Merrick is currently out of the office. She's on location setting up for an event."

Clara's grip on the phone tightened; she exchanged a glance with Derek, reading his silent encouragement.

"I understand. Can you tell me where she is?" Clara asked, the question laced with the gravity of their situation. "We really need to speak with her."

"Sure, she's at the Ritzmond Hotel. They're preparing for a gala tonight." The assistant's voice was infused with a touch of pride, unaware that each word painted a broader stroke in the grim portrait Clara was mentally assembling.

"Thank you, Heidi. That will be all," Clara said curtly before ending the call. She felt Derek's steady presence beside her as they gathered their things in silence, ready to confront yet another suspect who might hold the key to unraveling this mystery—or prove to be yet another dead end.

The drive to the Ritzmond Hotel was a silent one, punctuated only by the sound of the engine and the occasional blare of city traffic. Clara sat rigidly in her seat, her gaze fixed on the passing scenery, but her mind was elsewhere—trapped within the labyrinth of her own thoughts, retracing every step of the investigation.

As they approached, the Ritzmond Hotel loomed like a fortress of opulence against the skyline. Its grandiose façade, a testament to the wealth that flowed through its halls, stood in stark contrast to the darkness of their pursuit. Clara couldn't help but feel the dissonance between the hotel's exterior splendor and the internal decay of the crimes they sought to rectify.

"Think we'll find anything new here?" Derek finally broke the silence, his voice a low rumble that vibrated within the car's confined space.

"Every stone unturned is another opportunity," Clara replied, her tone even but her eyes betraying the skepticism that gnawed at her resolve. The hotel's valet opened her door with a flourish, a reminder of the world's continuous motion, indifferent to the suffering and chaos lurking beneath its surface.

They stepped onto the polished marble of the hotel's entryway, the air rich with the scent of luxury perfumed by money and power. Katherine Merrick was here somewhere, amid the finery and false smiles, and it was time to peel back the veneer of civility to reveal whether underneath lay the heart of a killer or just another bystander caught in the web of circumstance.

Clara stepped into the ballroom, her heels clicking softly on the polished parquet floor, a contrast to the thunderous beat of her heart. The room was a cavernous expanse of elegance and extravagance, lit by an army of crystal chandeliers that hung from the high ceiling like frozen teardrops of light. Long, heavy drapes in midnight blue pulled back with golden tassels framed vast windows, offering glimpses of the city's skyline as dusk began to drape its velvet cloak over the world outside.

The tables, dressed in pristine white linen, were adorned with centerpieces of exotic flowers whose petals unfurled with a languid grace, their vibrant colors waging a silent war against the room's grandeur. Silver cutlery lay in perfect symmetry beside delicate china, and each place setting was marked with a name card written in flourishing calligraphy. Clara noted the attention to detail, the signature of Katherine Merrick's handiwork.

In one corner of the room, a string quartet warmed up, playing a haunting melody, their bows drawing out notes that lingered in the air like whispered secrets. The music seemed to seep into Clara's bones, resonating with the tension that threaded through her muscles. She could feel Derek's presence behind her, a solid reassurance despite their earlier argument.

Glass sculptures, clear and fragile, caught the dying light and fractured it, sending shards of rainbows skating across walls and workers alike. It was a dance of light and shadow, a choreography that was meticulous and purposeful. Yet, for Clara, every shimmer held the potential of deception; every shadow could be a hiding place for darker truths.

They found Katherine Merrick overseeing the final touches near the stage, her keen eyes missing nothing. She was a woman who commanded the space around her, her posture radiating authority. Dressed in a sharp suit that matched the precision of her surroundings, she was the conductor of this symphony of social graces.

"Ms. Merrick?" Clara called out, her voice cutting through the din of preparations. Katherine turned, her expression one of mild surprise as she took in the sight of Clara and Derek, badges subtly displayed.

"Special Agent Pike, and this is my partner, Special Agent Morales. We need to ask you a few questions," Clara continued, her tone professional but not unkind.

Katherine's eyebrows rose slightly, a testament to her control that she did not let more surprise show. "Of course," she said smoothly, gesturing to a quieter spot away from the hustle of the event staff. "How can I help the FBI today?"

"We were hoping to speak with you about some recent murders," Derek began.

The ballroom's grandeur faded into a backdrop as Katherine Merrick's poised figure occupied Clara's focused attention. There was an air of refinement about her that seemed almost unassailable, but Clara had seen walls come down before—no facade was impenetrable.

"Your work must bring you to many interesting places," Clara began, the conversation a chess game where each piece moved with a precise objective. "As I understand it, two of them have recently been the site of serial murders."

Surprise registered in Katherine's eyes, a brief flicker before she composed herself. Her voice remained even as she replied, "I see. It is tragic what happened there. Such brutality in such beautiful spaces. But surely you don't think I'm involved?"

"Standard procedure," Derek chimed in, his tone suggesting routine while his eyes searched for any telltale sign of deception. "We just have to follow up with anyone who might have had extensive knowledge of the crime scenes."

"Of course," Katherine acquiesced with a nod, her demeanor cooperative yet guarded. "Ask away, then."

As they delved into their questions, Clara felt a twinge of doubt. Katherine's answers were smooth, rehearsed almost to perfection, yet there was no hint of evasion. She provided them with detailed accounts of her whereabouts on the days of the murders—alibis easily corroborated by witnesses and digital footprints. Clara's mind worked double-time trying to find a crack in Katherine's armor, but no crack could be found. Every instinct in Clara's body told her Katherine was telling the truth. She wasn't the killer, and both Clara and Derek knew it.

"It's a shame what happened," Katherine said wistfully. "Not just to those women but to the places themselves. I know it likely sounds silly to someone in your line of work, but I often get quite attached to the locations where I work. We spend so much of our lives at work, it's impossible for major moments not to happen there. That park, for example—it's where I met my husband. I heard my mother's voice for the last time during a phone call I took while working in that auditorium. I hate to think of them now, being the sites of such darkness."

Clara nodded. It was an interesting perspective. She had never really stopped to consider how much of her life might be tied to the buildings she spent her days in—how many personal moments had passed in those professional hallways.

"Thank you for your cooperation, Ms. Merrick," Derek said, having exhausted their list of questions. Clara knew disappointment lurked beneath his words, though he kept it from his voice.

Katherine offered a polite smile, the social veneer never slipping. "I hope you catch whoever is responsible," she said, her gaze steady. "It's a tragedy what happened."

"Indeed," Clara responded, her own smile more a mask than anything else. As they parted ways, her mind couldn't help but continue to sift through the details of Katherine's testimony, seeking a discrepancy that stubbornly refused to show itself.

Outside the hotel, the city breathed an undercurrent of secrets, and Clara felt the pull of countless unseen threads. Somewhere among them lay the key to the murders, but it was hidden well beyond her grasp. Katherine Merrick, despite all initial suspicions, had just faded into the background of potential leads, another shadow in the gallery of untouchable ghosts that haunted this case.

Clara's heels clicked against the pavement, a metronome to the thrumming disquiet in her chest. Each step away from the hotel felt like a descent deeper into the labyrinthine case that twisted before her and Derek with every turn. She glanced at her partner, his profile set in grim determination under the streetlights' watchful gaze.

"Grasping at straws," Clara murmured, more to herself than to him. Her voice was a low rush of air, barely audible above the city's hum—the distant wail of sirens, the chatter of pedestrians. "Even if her alibi wasn't rock solid, which it is, I still wouldn't buy her as a suspect. She's not our guy."

"Yeah." Derek sighed, his voice heavy, laden with the residue of their frustration. "But we had to check."

There was something in his tone that made Clara wonder if he really believed that or if he was just trying to convince himself. The truth was, the evidence that had led them to Katherine Merrick was incredibly thin, and they both knew it.

"It feels like we're missing something obvious—like it's right there in front of us," Clara said. Her mind scrolled through the day's events, snapshots of conversations and observations lining up, searching for a detail out of place. But before she could swim through that sea of data, the shrill ring of Derek's phone shattered her concentration.

Derek answered on the second ring, his expression shifting rapidly from weariness to alertness. Clara watched him, every muscle tensed, reading the change in his posture before he even spoke.

"Got it. We're on our way," he said tersely, ending the call. His eyes met Clara's, darkened by the news they carried. "There's been another murder."

The world seemed to still around them, the background noises fading into a muffled echo. Clara's heart pounded, the familiar surge of adrenaline flooding her system. The killer had made another move, shattering the brief illusion of calm and thrusting them back into the chase.

"Where?" Her voice was steady, the sharp edge of her resolve cutting through the haze.

"East end, near the docks. They'll need us to secure the scene."

Without another word, they got into the car, the engine coming to life with a roar that matched the sudden urgency pulsing between them. As Derek navigated through the streets, Clara stared out the window, the cityscape blurring past. Somewhere out there, amid the tangle of lives and lies, was a predator who remained shrouded in mystery—a mystery they were sworn to unravel, no matter the darkness they had to traverse. And with each victim claimed, the shadows grew denser around them, whispering of dangers unseen and the cost of every moment lost.

CHAPTER NINETEEN

Clara's breath clouded in the chilled air as she stepped out of the unmarked SUV and onto the damp pavement. The setting sun was a weak slash of orange against the gray sky, casting anemic light over the gym's façade. She could feel the weight of unseen eyes upon her —the specter of Lila Torres seemed to inhabit the very atmosphere, a silent witness to the horror that had unfolded within these walls mere hours before.

"Let's get this done," Derek muttered beside her, his face set in grim determination.

The front door of the gym creaked open with a disquieting moan, as if protesting their intrusion. Clara hesitated on the threshold, her senses heightening to absorb every detail. The assault on her olfactory nerves was immediate; the metallic tang of blood mingled with the musty scent of sweat-soaked mats.

She advanced cautiously into the cavernous space, heels clicking on the polished floor. Sunbeams slipped through high windows, casting long shadows that seemed to stretch out like grasping fingers. The gym was eerily silent but for the distant hum of fluorescent lights, a stark contrast to the cacophony of exertion that would normally fill it.

As they moved deeper into the facility, past rows of dormant balance beams and high bars, Clara's gaze zeroed in on the far corner where yellow tape fluttered like grim pennants marking the crime scene.

She made her way to the small storage closet, Derek following close behind. There, amidst chalk bins and trampolines, lay the epicenter of violence.

"Looks like quite a struggle took place here," Derek observed.

Clara nodded, squatting by a set of skid marks on the matting. They were disjointed and chaotic, telling a silent tale of desperation and fight. Her eyes trailed to the wall nearby, noting a splotch of darker hue that stood out against the sterile whiteness—a handprint smeared in a downward slide. Blood, no doubt, from Lila's final moments.

"Defensive wounds, maybe?" Clara mused aloud, touching the edge of the print with the tip of her pen. "She fought back hard."

"Tracks with what we know about her," Derek replied. "Athletic, strong…she wouldn't have gone down easily."

The evidence of a struggle was undeniable. Scuff marks disturbed the otherwise pristine floor, and a tub of chalk had been toppled over, seemingly mid-lift. It was easy to imagine Lila's powerful frame grappling with an assailant, her muscles honed by years of training now employed in a desperate bid for survival. The killer likely had the element of surprise. If he hadn't, who knows how this would have ended.

"Too bad strength alone isn't enough when you're taken by surprise," Clara said, her voice tinged with sorrow for the life so brutally extinguished.

"Let's hope she left us something to go on," Derek added, scanning the area for additional clues.

Clara stood, surveying the chaos. She could almost hear the echoes of struggle, the heavy breaths, the grunts of exertion. In her mind's eye, Lila was there, fighting for her life. With a shiver, Clara refocused on the present, aware that Lila's ghost would haunt her until justice was served.

The setting sun spilled through the high windows of the gym, casting elongated shadows that seemed to dance across the crime scene tape. Clara Pike stood just outside the halo of light, her gaze fixed on the splatters of blood on the wall. The time stamp on Lila Torres's murder was at odds with the nighttime pattern of the previous killings.

"Daylight," Derek said, breaking into Clara's thoughts. "That's new."

Clara nodded, her gaze still locked on the gruesome tableau. "He's escalating, getting bolder. Or maybe he's just adapting to our moves."

"Could be he's feeling the heat, getting nervous," Derek suggested, surveying the perimeter with a critical eye. "Or it's possible he wanted to send a message by choosing broad daylight for his stage."

"Either way, it's a deviation we can't ignore." Clara's voice was grave. "Forensics will give us the timeline, but the why is what troubles me. Why take the risk of a daytime hit in a public place?"

"Desperation? A personal vendetta?" Derek paced slowly, hands clasped behind his back. "Or he's evolving, which means we have to as well."

"Let's see what the last person to see Lila alive has to say about today's events." Clara motioned toward the entrance, where a young woman sat on a bench, her posture rigid with shock and grief.

They approached the co-worker, whose eyes were red-rimmed and distant. "I'm sorry to bother you, but I'm Special Agent Pike, and this is my partner, Special Agent Morales. You knew Lila Torres?"

The woman nodded, her lips quivering. "I saw her this morning. She was opening up as usual. We exchanged a few words about a student's progress."

"Did you notice anything unusual? Anyone around who shouldn't have been?" Clara asked, her tone gentle but insistent.

The woman shook her head slowly. "No, it was just a normal day until… until it wasn't." She swallowed hard, fighting back tears. "Lila was always the first one here. Dedicated, you know? It doesn't make sense."

"Can you think of anyone who might have held a grudge against her? Any recent altercations or threats?" Derek inquired, his eyes searching the woman's face for any flicker of recognition.

"Nothing like that. Lila was friendly, professional. Everyone loved her." Her voice cracked, and she took a moment to compose herself. "She was a hell of a gymnast back in the day. On track for the Olympics. Everyone felt really lucky to get to train with someone of her caliber."

"Is there anything else you can think of? Anything at all we should know?" Clara asked, but the woman just shook her head, tears threatening to overcome her.

"That's okay. We appreciate you speaking with us," Clara said, handing over her card. "If you remember anything else, anything at all, please call me."

"Jessica and Naomi," Clara said, as she and Derek moved through the crime scene. "They both died where their worst memories lived. But Cassie and Lila, it's different for them."

Derek looked up at her, his dark eyes somber. "Yeah, for them, it was just their places of employment. No apparent emotional trauma tied to the location. It's odd. I would expect more consistency."

Clara walked beside a vaulting table and then made her way past a pommel horse.

"It's as if he wants us to see a pattern," she mused, "but then he breaks it just enough to keep us guessing."

"Could be his way of taunting us," Derek suggested as they made their way past a tumbling mat. His hands rested on his hips as he surveyed the scene. "Or maybe he's evolving, getting more brazen with each kill."

"Evolution suggests progression, learning," Clara countered, her gaze fixated on the textured grip of the dumbbells nearby. "But this feels like… deviation. A deliberate step sideways."

"Maybe that's the point," Derek proposed, his expression hardening. "To throw us off, make us question everything we thought we knew."

They moved synchronously through the space, their trained eyes scanning for anything out of place. Clara's photographic memory cataloged every detail as though it was a silent witness, holding its secrets close. Soaking it all in was key. In investigations, it wasn't at all uncommon for agents to have to visit the crime scene multiple times as their theories developed, or to be stuck looking at pictures that didn't tell the whole story. If she took it all in now, she could save them from both of those things, which would make their investigation far more efficient and effective. And with a serial killer on the loose, time and expediency were of the essence.

"Clara?" Derek's voice pulled her back to the present. She looked up to find him standing near the entrance, his silhouette framed by the dying light. She was surprised to see him there. She'd been so absorbed in surveying the scene that she hadn't even noticed he was no longer standing beside her.

"Coming," Clara said, her eyes scanning the gym one last time before heading toward the exit. Together, they stepped out of the gym, leaving the silence behind as they ventured back into the clamor of the living, carrying with them the weight of the dead and their untold stories.

Clara's mind was a whirling dervish of facts and hunches as she navigated the SUV through the thickening twilight. The day had been mercilessly long, and now, as night descended, the city's lights flickered on, casting long shadows and painting the streets with an eerie glow.

"Something isn't adding up," Clara murmured, her grip tightening on the steering wheel. Beside her, Derek remained silent, his profile etched in contemplation against the passing street lamps.

"Remember what Katherine Merrick said about the locations—how so much of our lives happen at work? Maybe there's more to Lila's and Cassie's relationships with their crime scenes than them being their places of employment. Just because we haven't seen a deeper connection yet doesn't mean it isn't there."

"I think you're right," Derek replied. "We're missing something crucial about these locations. The killer chose them for a reason. His pattern is too deliberate. So maybe that's the key. Maybe these locations meant more to them than we know. Hidden memories or experiences tied to their pasts."

"Exactly," Clara said, feeling the first tendrils of excitement. "We need to uncover those hidden strands. We assumed these spaces are simply where they were employed, but what if they're not? What if they're carefully chosen stages for a final act?"

"Stages," Derek echoed, the word hanging between them like a challenge. They both knew the answer lay within the victims' histories, their personal narratives that had somehow led them to be chosen by a meticulous killer. The pieces of the puzzle were there, scattered and elusive, waiting to be connected.

"Let's speak with Lila's parents," Clara decided, her voice laced with determination. "They might hold the key to understanding her true relationship with the gym."

Derek nodded, and Clara felt her resolve harden. They would peel back the layers of Lila's life until they unearthed the truth, no matter how deep it was buried. She accelerated into the night, the darkness ahead holding both the promise of answers and the threat of more questions.

CHAPTER TWENTY

The Torres residence loomed before them, its facade a stoic testament to the family that resided within. Clara hesitated on the doorstep, collecting her thoughts. Past experiences had taught her that the homes of the bereaved held an atmosphere thick with grief—a tangible presence that clung to one's skin.

The door loomed before them, a barrier to both the known and the unknowable. Clara's hand moved almost mechanically to announce their arrival. The sound of her knock seemed to resonate deeper than the thick oak it reverberated against, echoing into the cavernous space where anticipation and dread coexisted.

In this moment, Clara Pike was not just an FBI agent; she was a silent witness to the echoing agony of families torn apart by the cruelties of fate. And as she waited for the door to open, she steadied herself with the knowledge that each piece of the puzzle she uncovered brought her one step closer to understanding, to preventing another doorway from becoming a portal to someone else's despair.

A soft shuffle from within preceded the click of a latch. The door swung inward, revealing the strained faces of Lila Torres's parents, Ana and Jorge. Their eyes were rimmed with red, a testament to countless tears shed, their expressions etched with the raw mark of loss—a look Clara knew all too well.

"Hello, Mr. and Mrs. Torres. I'm FBI Special Agent Derek Morales," Derek began, "and this is my partner, Special Agent Clara Pike. We're so sorry to disturb you, especially this late. But we were hoping to speak with you about Lila."

"Of course. Please come in," Lila's mother managed, her voice a fragile whisper that barely carried over the threshold. They stepped inside, enveloped immediately by the scent of brewed coffee and faded perfume—the olfactory echoes of routine and memory colliding with tragedy.

The living room held onto the faded echoes of better days, its walls adorned with family portraits smiling from a past that felt irretrievable. Amidst the normalcy of thrown cushions and half-read books, the somber reality of their visit cast a shadow that seemed to darken every corner.

As they were ushered to a couch that faced a mantel crowded with Lila's accolades—a stark reminder of dreams dashed—Clara took in the muted tones of the room. The light filtering through the window blinds sliced the air into slats of gold and gray, painting the grief in starker contrast. Here, in this sanctum of sorrow, they would seek answers, gently prying open wounds in hopes of finding the key to a puzzle that had claimed too many lives already.

Derek sat beside her, his body language open yet respectful, ready to navigate the delicate balance between empathy and inquiry. In the quiet that followed their seating, Clara felt the weight of every word they were about to speak. Each question might offer solace, or it could add another brick to the barricade of pain. As the silence stretched, she locked eyes with Lila's mother, and without a word, vowed to find the truth that might someday set them all free.

Clara brushed a strand of hair behind her ear, a subtle stalling gesture as she prepared herself to breach the chasm of grief that lay before them. The room's stillness was disquieting, an eerie prelude to the storm of emotions they were about to stir. Lila's parents sat opposite them, two figures carved from pain and loss, holding each other's hands like lifelines in this sea of sorrow.

"Mr. and Mrs. Torres," Clara began, her voice a gentle timbre amidst the silence, "we cannot fathom the depth of your loss, but we are here to help find justice for Lila." She paused, giving space for her words to settle, for the parents' numb expressions to register her intent. It was a delicate dance—one wrong step and the fragile trust could shatter.

"Can you tell us about Lila?" Derek interjected smoothly, his tone one of careful curiosity rather than interrogation. "What was she like?"

Lila's mother drew in a breath, her lips quivering as if summoning the strength to speak would withdraw the last reserves of her fortitude. "Lila… she was light," she said, her voice quavering. "Always moving, always laughing. She loved her work, loved helping others find their strength."

"Her energy was infectious," her father added, his voice a stark contrast, hollowed out by despair. "She put everything into her coaching—her passion was undeniable."

The room seemed to breathe with Lila's memory, echoes of her vivacity lingering in the corners where shadows converged, whispering secrets that only the walls had borne witness to.

"Did Lila have any particular connection to the gym where she… where she was found?" Clara asked, treading carefully, watching as Lila's parents exchanged a glance heavy with unspoken words.

"Beyond her job as a coach there?" Derek clarified, leaning forward slightly, his eyes intent on capturing every nuance of their response.

The question hung in the air, a specter waiting to be clothed in truth. Lila's mother's gaze drifted toward the mantelpiece, to a photograph of a younger Lila, poised in graceful balance on a beam, her smile triumphant and full of promise.

"She was always at that gym," her mother whispered, the memories seeming to cascade over her like a tangible veil. "Since she was a little girl, tumbling mats and chalk dust were her world. When she wasn't coaching…" Her voice trailed off, and Clara knew they were edging closer to an abyss of revelation, the precipice that might lead them to the heart of the darkness they sought to unveil.

Clara's fingers curled around the edges of her notepad, the paper crackling softly under the tension. Lila's mother steadied herself against the armrests of her chair, a silent sentinel amidst the storm of grief. "Lila… she grew up in that gym," she finally continued, her voice a fraying thread in the quiet room. "She was a deeply gifted gymnast. Good at the power stuff, but graceful, too. One of those rare gymnasts who's every bit as good on the bars as she was on the floor. She was four the first time she told me she was going to be in the Olympics someday. At the time, it seemed like a childish flight of fancy, but by the time she was fourteen…"

Ana swallowed hard, taking a moment to gather herself. Clara could tell it pained her, but she continued anyway.

"She was nationally ranked. They were expecting her to make the world championship team the next year. And then, one day, she was working on a new vault, and she just landed wrong. Total freak accident, but it tore her ACL completely."

"Her career ended right there," Lila's father added, his voice laced with a bitterness that seemed at odds with the softness in his eyes as he regarded the image of his daughter. "She sank into a deep depression after that. We couldn't get her interested in anything. She refused to go back into the gym. Wouldn't do her schoolwork. If she couldn't be in the Olympics, she didn't want to do anything at all."

"We tried to be patient," Ana continued, but Jorge jumped back in.

"But we couldn't let her just waste her life. So, when she turned eighteen, we told her she had a choice: get a job, get an education, or get out. The problem was she wasn't actually qualified to do anything except gymnastics."

"But the owners of the gym," Ana began, "they loved Lila. Always had. After her injury, they offered her a coaching position, but she refused it at the time. But after getting rejected from everywhere up to and including McDonald's and Walmart, she decided to go back and ask if the offer still stood."

"And I take it it did?" Clara asked.

"She never got over the loss of her competitive career, but she found a new love in coaching. She poured her heart into those students, in spite of the pain it sometimes caused her to watch them. Tried to give others the chance she lost."

Derek shifted, his posture respectful but his profiler's mind undoubtedly cataloging every word, every twitch of their faces. Clara felt the puzzle pieces clicking together, forming a picture more complex than they had anticipated. A location tied directly to the most pivotal and painful moment of their victim's life—just like Jessica and Naomi. It couldn't be coincidence.

"Thank you," Clara said, her voice measured but gentle, acknowledging the pain that clung to the words like ivy to an aging wall. "We appreciate you sharing this with us. It helps more than you know."

Lila's parents nodded, weariness etched into their features. They rose slowly, the motion seeming to take everything they had left. Derek offered a hand, which Lila's father grasped firmly, a silent message of gratitude passing between them. Clara tucked her notepad away, her mind racing with implications, but her face remained a mask of professional calm.

"Goodbye, Mrs. Torres, Mr. Torres," Derek said, with a nod toward Lila's parents. "If you think of anything else that may be relevant to the investigation, please don't hesitate to get in touch."

"Of course," Ana replied as she opened the door for them. As Clara and Derek reached the sidewalk, they heard Ana's voice behind them.

"Please," she called out, her voice breaking on the word, "find who did this to our girl."

"We will," Clara affirmed, though the promise tasted bitter on her tongue.

"We'll do everything we can," Derek swiftly added.

Together, they stepped across the threshold, feeling the finality of the door closing behind them, sealing them away from the sanctuary of grief.

Outside, the sky was a canvas of grays and blacks, clouds looming ominously overhead as if mirroring the turbulence within Clara's thoughts. She breathed in the crisp air, trying to dispel the claustrophobia of despair that clung to the walls of the house they'd just exited.

"Let's go," Derek murmured, his eyes scanning the horizon as if searching for an omen. Clara nodded, her mind already weaving through the labyrinth of details they had amassed. Each fact, each spoken word, was another stitch in the tapestry of tragedy and determination that she carried within her.

"Would you mind driving?" she asked Derek, her voice steady despite the whirlwind inside her. "I think I need to make a call."

"Who to?" Derek asked. "And before you try and obfuscate, remember, I'm a profiler for the FBI. So I am very, very good at getting people to tell me the truth."

"Cassie Marlowe's sister," Clara replied. "I've got a hunch I want to run down."

***

Clara's hand trembled slightly as she reached for her phone, the device suddenly feeling like a leaden weight in her palm. She punched in the number with mechanical precision, her mind ticking over the facts that now seemed to bind together with an eerie significance.

When Cassie's sister, Jennifer, picked up, a surge of adrenaline rushed through Clara's body.

"Hi, Jennifer," Clara began, doing her best to keep her voice steady. This is Special Agent Clara Pike with the FBI." The silence around her was punctuated only by the distant hum of traffic and the faint rustle of leaves in the breeze.

"We know Cassie was killed at her place of employment and that she had been a student there, but we don't know much about her experience in either of those roles. We were hoping you could help us with that."

"Of course," Jennifer said, her voice shaking slightly. "Whatever you need."

"Do you happen to know if Cassie experienced any sort of trauma there, either as a teacher or a student?" Clara asked.

There was a pause on the line, a momentary hitch in the rhythm of their investigation. Then came the confirmation, delivered with a tremble that resonated with loss and old pain. "Yes, her best friend died during our senior year. Rachel… she hung herself in the school auditorium. Cassie was the one who found the body."

"I have to imagine that was deeply traumatizing," Clara offered.

"It was," Jennifer replied. "For a while, she swore she'd never step foot in that building again. She couldn't even go near the auditorium without having a panic attack. But when her old drama teacher retired and asked her to take over—well, she surprised us all by saying yes. She said she wanted to use her position to provide a safe place for students. She wanted to do it for Rachel."

Clara closed her eyes, allowing the photographic details to snap into place with unnerving clarity. The auditorium where Cassie's body had been found, her life extinguished amidst the echoes of children's laughter and the squeak of rubber-soled shoes on polished wood. A former stage for triumphs and heartbreak had turned into a tableau of death.

"Thank you," Clara murmured.

She ended the call and looked at Derek, her gaze laden with the gravity of their discovery.

Derek nodded, his jaw set firm with newfound resolve. They stood side by side, their profiles etched against the encroaching gloom of the day, two silhouettes bound by duty and the relentless pursuit of justice.

"Victimology," Derek said, breaking the silence. "We've got a pattern."

"Highly personal locations," Clara added, her brain whirring into overdrive. "Places of profound pain and loss."

The profile was becoming clearer with each revelation, each uncovered secret—a killer targeting victims in places that represented their deepest sorrows, turning sanctuaries of memory into gravesites.

But even with the profile fleshed out, the specter of the unknown loomed large. They were piecing together the why but still grappling with the who. The killer remained a ghost in the machine of their case, a shadow slipping through their fingers with infuriating ease.

"Where do we go from here?" Derek asked, his voice cutting through Clara's contemplation.

"More digging," Clara replied, resolute, despite the frustration gnawing at her insides. "Patterns are only part of the puzzle. We need a name, a face…"

"Something we can chase," Derek finished for her.

They turned back toward the car, their movements synchronized, each step carrying the weight of their mission. The air was thick with the promise of rain, the imminent downpour a fitting metaphor for the deluge of revelations they hoped to uncover.

Yet, amidst the certainty of their profiling expertise, doubt whispered through the cracks of their confidence. With every victim woven so intimately into the tapestry of their demise, the unseen hand that wrought such destruction felt closer than ever—yet just beyond reach. The realization settled over Clara with chilling familiarity, a reminder of the answers that sometimes refused to be found.

CHAPTER TWENTY ONE

Clara Pike stood motionless in the dimly lit records room, surrounded by towering shelves of case files, her eyes fixated on a map splayed out before her. Red pins dotted the cityscape, each marking the last breaths of the victims, a morbid constellation that seemed to reveal both everything and nothing at all. The air was thick with the scent of aging paper and the faint musk of mildew—an olfactory reminder of the decay that clung to the unsolved and the forgotten.

She traced a line from one pin to the next with a slender finger, her heart heavy with the revelation that each woman had been found at the site of some past personal hell. It felt like a breakthrough, this pattern of historical wounds reopened, but every lead seemed to wither under her scrutiny, as elusive as the shadow of the perpetrator she hunted.

"Hey." Derek's voice cut through the silence, and Clara flinched slightly, drawn out from her tunnel vision of despair. He leaned against the steel door frame, his brow creased with concern. "You doing okay? You've been tracing that line for like five minutes."

"Feels like I'm getting nowhere, Derek," Clara muttered, her photographic memory replaying the interviews with the families—each filled with anguish, each a dead end in disguise. She couldn't shake the image of Lila's mother, a damn of tears held back with duct tape and glue, or Jessica's sister, stone-faced but eyes betraying a storm of unspoken pain.

"Sometimes the answer isn't in what we see, but in what we don't," Derek said, stepping into the room, his presence a grounding force amidst the chaos. "Look, Clara, it's different for you. You see everything all of the time, and that would be draining for anyone. Maybe you need to step back for a bit. Clear your head."

"Every minute I'm not working is another moment the killer is out there, unstopped," Clara replied, her voice sharpened by frustration. Yet, somewhere beneath the layers of fatigue and obsession, she knew Derek's counsel held weight. In the rare moments when she allowed herself reprieve from the case, a new angle would often materialize, as if her subconscious continued to work while she consciously retreated.

Derek approached and placed a gentle hand on her shoulder. "Look, Clara, the reality is the killer is out there, and he's going to do whatever he's going to do whether you run yourself into the ground or not. I know it's tough, but trust me on this. We've been at this non-stop. A break could be exactly what you need to find a different angle."

The suggestion hung between them like a lifeline she was hesitant to grab onto. But Derek understood the toll cases took on her, how she became ensnared by the minutiae others easily overlooked. He respected her abilities, yet also knew when to pull her back from the precipice of her own mind.

"I'll hold down the fort here," he added. "I promise."

"Alright," she conceded with a reluctant nod, her gaze lingering on the map. "But only for a little while." Derek offered her a small, reassuring smile, the kind that acknowledged the depth of her dedication and the shared burden of their quest for justice.

"Promise me you'll try to relax," he said, knowing full well the challenge he presented her.

"I'll do my best," Clara answered, though they both understood that for her, stepping away from the case was akin to leaving a part of herself behind in the darkness of the records room.

She honored that promise, doing everything she could to disconnect as she climbed in the car and began navigating the city streets, but nothing seemed to be working. Her knuckles whitened as she gripped the steering wheel, the leather creaking under the strain. The weight of the case pressed on her from all sides, suffocating in its intensity. Her mind was a maelstrom of crime scene photos and victim statements, swirling with the haunting sense that each woman's past had somehow sealed her fate.

The city receded in her rearview mirror as she drove, houses blurring into indistinct shapes against the encroaching dusk. Derek's words resonated in her thoughts, a mantra urging her to distance herself, if only for a moment. She was resistant, her instincts screaming to stay, to dig deeper, yet the part of her that still clung to reason knew he was right. The pattern was there, hidden beneath layers of trauma and fear; she just needed to step back to see it.

Clearing her head had always been akin to navigating through fog—difficult, but not impossible. Every breakthrough in previous cases had come after these calculated retreats, though they never felt natural or welcome. As much as her spirit rebelled against the notion of rest, she couldn't deny the effectiveness of stepping back to leap forward.

The city lights began to twinkle on, stars igniting one by one in the twilight of the urban landscape. Trust was not given easily in her line of work, but Derek had earned his share. She trusted him to handle the legwork, to keep the investigation moving while she sought temporary refuge from the storm in her mind.

She pulled off the main road, parking in a secluded lot overlooking the river where it flowed dark and inscrutable beneath the burgeoning night. With a sigh, she reached for her phone, the device cold and impersonal in her hand. Clara dialed Jack Sullivan's number, the familiar sequence of digits offering an anchor in the tumult.

"Jack," she greeted as the call connected, her voice betraying none of the chaos within. "It's Clara."

"Clara! What can I do for you?" His voice was gravelly but warm, a comforting sound amidst her disquiet.

"Can we meet? I need to talk—the case is… it's a mess inside my head."

"Of course," Jack replied without hesitation, the underlying concern evident even through the phone. "I'm at the rowing club, down by the Potomac. Head over here?"

"Give me twenty minutes," Clara said, already feeling the tentative threads of a plan weaving together in the recesses of her mind. Jack had always been able to cut through the noise, helping her refocus when the details threatened to overwhelm her sense of the whole.

"See you soon," Jack said before ending the call.

***

The Potomac River unfurled like a dark ribbon under the fading light, its surface reflecting the last embers of twilight. Clara's shoes crunched on the gravel path leading to the boathouse where Jack said he'd be. Her eyes, sharp as a hawk's, scanned the area, instinctively cataloging everything—the way the willows draped over the water like mournful spectators, the rhythmic chirp of crickets, and the distant silhouette of Jack Sullivan unloading his scull from the rack.

"Clara!" Jack called out, his voice sturdy as oak, breaking through the dusky haze. "Over here!"

She approached, her mind still whirring with fragments of the case, each piece refusing to click into place. The air was heavy with mist, laden with the scent of damp earth and river water. Jack stood beside the slender boat, the muscles in his forearms visible as he secured an oar.

"Thought you'd find me at a desk?" He grinned, the lines around his eyes deepening—a map of all the years he'd spent mentoring agents like her. "Come on," he beckoned, his tone brooking no argument, "let's get you set up."

"Jack, I don't think—" she started, but he cut her off.

"Clara, trust me. There's something about being on the water, it's meditative. Helps clear the mind." He handed her a life jacket, his gaze unwavering, understanding her resistance yet gently pushing past it.

"Fine," she conceded, her hands moving to fit the life jacket snugly around her torso. She could never truly say no to Jack; the man had an uncanny ability to know what she needed before she did.

They slid the scull into the Potomac with practiced ease, the vessel barely causing a ripple. As they settled into the shell, the boat wobbled slightly under their combined weight, demanding balance and focus—a welcome distraction.

"Ready?" Jack asked, handing her the oars. His voice held that same steadiness that had guided her through training drills back at Quantico.

"Always," Clara responded, though her grip on the oars betrayed a slight tremor. She dipped the blades into the water, feeling the cool rush against her skin, the current eager to sweep them along.

With each stroke, they carved through the liquid night, leaving behind a frothy trail. The rhythm of rowing, the push and pull, became a metronome for her thoughts. Trees lined the bank, their shadows stretching toward them like fingers trying to snatch at the secrets she harbored.

"Talk to me, Clara," Jack urged, his strokes mirroring hers as they found their pace. His voice was both a tether and a lifeline in the growing darkness. She opened her mouth to speak, but the words lodged in her throat, heavy and unformed.

"Take your time," he reassured her, patient as the tide. They moved together, synchronized in silence, until finally, Clara began to unravel the knot of details that plagued her mind.

The oars sliced through the water with mechanical precision, each stroke propelling them further into the calm expanse of the Potomac. Silver moonlight danced on the surface, illuminating their path like shards of a shattered mirror. Clara Pike concentrated on the rhythm, the repetitive motion that seemed to churn the fog in her mind into something more lucid.

"This killer," she began finally, voice steady despite the exertion, "targets locations tied to the victims' past traumas. It's... personal for him." She noted how the river seemed to swallow her words as if absorbing the gravity of her investigation.

"Like he's taunting them with their own histories," she continued, the oars plunging and rising, a physical metaphor for the dive into the victims' lives she had taken. The darkness of the water below mirrored the abyss of the case that threatened to consume her.

"Each woman, reliving a nightmare before…" Her sentence trailed off, the reality too harsh to voice aloud against the serenity of the night. Instead, she focused on the oars, the only sound the rhythmic splash and recovery as they cut through the blackness.

Jack rowed in silence behind her, letting her words ripple out, giving space for the tension to unravel from Clara's shoulders. He understood the weight of the case on her, saw the familiar furrow in her brow that signaled wheels turning relentlessly within.

The boat glided onward, and Clara felt something shift inside her—a loosening of the mental knots as the physical ones tightened in her muscles. The clarity she sought was here somewhere, between the strokes and the whispers of the river.

"Clara." Jack's voice sliced through the cadence of their strokes. "You're chasing shadows in the same darkness that he is. You need to step into the light."

She paused, mid-stroke, feeling the boat's momentum carry them forward as her arms hovered in suspension. Jack's eyes met hers, reflecting a wisdom hardened by years of navigating cases that wound like the river—unpredictable and deep.

"Consider the connections between these women, not just their pasts," he suggested. His tone wasn't dismissive but redirecting, an attempt to steer her investigative compass toward uncharted territories.

"Connections?" Clara echoed, lowering the oars back into the water, the gentle splash punctuating her uncertainty.

"There's something that binds them besides their trauma. Or, at least, in addition to it. The trauma may be why the killer is choosing these victims, but it's not the how. You need to find the common thread, Clara." Jack's instruction was simple yet daunting. "Sometimes, it's not about the pain they suffered but about who might have woven those moments together."

As they resumed rowing, the idea took hold, growing roots in the fertile ground of her thoughts. The movement of their bodies, the symphony of action and reflection, became a dance of possibility. Could there be a pivot point, a singular nexus that bound these women?

"Focus on the here and now, on what ties them together today," Jack advised, his gaze never leaving the water ahead. His words were like a beacon, guiding her away from the lure of the past's siren call.

Clara nodded, her mind racing as she dissected every interview, every crime scene photo, every report she'd memorized. The connection was there, she was sure of it; it just needed to be unearthed from the tangled web of her recollections.

The boat continued its journey, a speck of determination amidst the vastness, with Clara at the helm, steering toward revelation.

CHAPTER TWENTY TWO

The dashboard clock's neon digits cut through the dimness, declaring it just past eight o'clock. The night was a cocoon of silence inside his car, except for the soft purr of the engine as he sat parked in the shadowed alleyway. His eyes, sharp and calculating, were fixed on the entrance of a plush downtown office building where the fluorescent lights within cast long, distorted shadows onto the pavement outside. He adjusted the rearview mirror, not to gaze upon himself but to survey the street behind him—a mere precaution in his meticulous plan.

The killer's hands gripped the steering wheel with an intensity that would leave most knuckles white, but his were unfazed—practiced in the art of restraint. Every minute that passed was a testament to his patience, a virtue he cultivated like a rare orchid in the garden of his twisted resolve. Valerie Hudson had become an obsession, a challenge he could neither abandon nor overcome with haste.

He watched as she finally emerged, her silhouette unmistakable even at this distance. There was something about her that took him back to another place and time. To a house he longed to escape with a woman who would never be brave enough to leave.

The killer's breath caught in his throat, a reaction involuntary and rare, as she approached the car. Valerie had frustrated him unlike any other before her. Cassie, Jessica, Naomi, Lila—they had all been so susceptible to his manipulative whispers, so amenable to his suggestions that preyed on their vulnerabilities. But not Valerie. She held firm, resistant to the lures he dangled before her, blind to the breadcrumbs he laid out that should have led her back to the courtroom where her life had once splintered into fragments of despair.

"Stubborn," he muttered to himself. Just like his mother. No amount of persuasion was ever going to get her to move. But no matter. He would make her move. If she wasn't willing to return to the place of her greatest trauma, the place he yearned to make the stage for his grand finale on her own accord, he would simply have to take her there.

As Valerie's car keys jingled, a sound barely audible from his vantage point, his mind raced with possibilities. With a slow intake of breath, he started his car, the headlights remaining off as he coasted out of the alleyway with predatory stealth. The chase was not yet over, and the night still held promises that only he could fulfill. As he followed at a discreet distance, shadows cloaked his vehicle, rendering it no more than a phantom whisper trailing behind Valerie Hudson's unsuspecting steps.

The engine hummed a low dirge as he pulled into the same rhythm of the city's nocturnal pulse. He followed her into a parking garage, where her taillights were beacons in the murky depths, a red allure guiding him through the concrete labyrinth. The air was thick with the scent of exhaust and the faint whiff of refuse from nearby bins. Each level he ascended tightened the coil of anticipation within him.

His fingers curled tighter around the steering wheel, a silent vow etched into the grooves of his skin. It wasn't merely a desire that tethered him to this pursuit—it was an imperative. A compulsion carved from the bedrock of his purpose.

The fluorescent lights flickered overhead, casting stroboscopic shadows that danced across the killer's face, now etched with resolve. He eased his car into a crawl, eyes never straying from the silhouette of Valerie's vehicle.

With each turn of the wheels, the space between them seemed to shrink, not just in physical distance but in the narrowing gap of inevitability. The parking garage welcomed him with open arms, a concrete behemoth that held within its walls secrets and sins alike. The dull echo of his tires against the ramp resonated like a drumbeat, a harbinger of the endgame that drew near. He could sense Valerie's presence ahead, moving ever closer to her unwitting destiny.

This was no sterile hunting ground; the garage bore the patina of urban decay and the weariness of countless homecomings. But tonight, it would serve as the backdrop for something altogether different—an encounter ordained by a twisted sense of justice. His heartbeat synchronized with the thrum of the engine, each pulse a step closer to the culmination of his grand design.

Valerie's car came to a stop, and the gentle purr of her engine dying was like the last sigh of day yielding to night. He brought his vehicle to rest at a calculated distance, where his hands lay steady on the steering wheel, the leather cool and unyielding beneath his fingers. His gaze, sharp and unwavering, followed Valerie's silhouette as she gathered her belongings, seemingly oblivious to the hunter just a car's breadth away. Every cell in his body was attuned to her movements; he had studied her, knew her routines like verses of an unholy scripture. The parking garage around them was a cavernous expanse of concrete and shadow, a quiet mausoleum for vehicles that now also concealed a predator.

Valerie's door opened, its creak a whisper lost in the void between the walls. He mirrored her actions, the click of his own door barely audible as he stepped onto the coarse cement floor. His feet made no sound, his steps practiced and precise—he was a ghost, a wraith clad in the garb of mundane humanity. The dim glow from the overhead lights cast pools of luminance amidst the darkness, painting stark contrasts over the dusty ground like spotlights awaiting their cue in this macabre drama.

The air was laced with the scent of oil and rubber, the tang of metal faintly rusting in the stale atmosphere. It was a place forgotten by time and warmth, where echoes were swallowed whole and secrets kept. His heart thrummed a low, rhythmic dirge against his ribcage, but his exterior betrayed none of the fervor that coursed through him. This was it—the moment before the plunge, the intake of breath before the descent into the abyss of his own making.

Valerie shut her car door with a soft click, sealing herself off from the sanctuary of her vehicle. Unaware of the danger lurking so close, she locked the door, the beep of her alarm echoing like a distant siren call. The killer watched her, every fiber of his being coiled tight with anticipation. He stood there, a silent sentry, waiting for the precise moment to step out of the shadows and into her life.

She turned, her footsteps a soft patter against the brutalist canvas of the garage. The killer moved with a fluid grace, a shadow slipping through the dimness of the concrete jungle. As he crept closer, each footfall was calculated, a deliberate dance with destiny that had been choreographed in the dark recesses of his twisted mind. This was more than a hunt; it was a pilgrimage, and Valerie Hudson was the unwitting deity at its end.

And then, he was behind her, close enough to discern the subtle floral notes of her perfume—a stark contrast to the mustiness of their surroundings. The proximity was intoxicating, the culmination of obsessive longing, and he savored the fleeting seconds as time seemed to distort, stretching the fibers of reality thin. She was unaware, still encased in the fragile bubble of her daily routine, her senses dulled to the predator that shared her space.

His presence was an invisible force, a palpable tension in the air that screamed warnings left unheard. The silence of the killer was a testament to his dedication, to the countless hours he had spent perfecting his approach, honing his craft until he became the very essence of stealth and surprise. In the desolate expanse of the garage, with only the faint hum of distant traffic as a backdrop, he waited for the inevitable moment to strike, his resolve as unshakeable as the concrete pillars that surrounded them.

Valerie fumbled with her keys, a clink of metal against metal piercing the quiet. She never saw him move, never sensed the looming danger as he closed the distance between them. With the precision of a shadow merging with the night, he struck, hand sweeping over her mouth, the chloroform-soaked fabric sealing her fate. Her eyes widened, a flash of terror igniting within their depths, but her scream was suffocated, smothered before it could birth into existence.

He felt her struggle, a fluttering bird trapped within his unyielding grasp, but the chloroform was relentless, a chemical reaper harvesting consciousness. Her body slackened, her fight draining away as if someone had pulled the plug on her very soul. He caught her limp form, cradling her in arms that were both captor and savior, her weight a confirmation of his control, of the inevitability he had orchestrated.

With acute awareness, he scanned the desolate levels of the garage, his senses attuned to any hint of intrusion. There was only the hushed echo of distant footsteps, likely belonging to some late-night office worker oblivious to the dark theatre unfolding in their midst. Assured of their solitude, he moved toward his car, his burden now a precious cargo that held the key to his twisted salvation.

The vehicle, a nondescript sedan that blended with the shadows, waited with doors unlocked, a silent accomplice to his cause. Gently, with an almost reverent touch, he placed Valerie into the backseat. His movements were fluid, the practiced ease of one who had played this scene many times before in the recesses of his mind. The leather creaked softly under her weight, the only sound in the void as he positioned her with meticulous care.

His actions were swift, yet unhurried—time was his ally, and he wielded it with the finesse of a master craftsman. He ensured she lay undisturbed, an unsuspecting guest on the velvet stage of unconsciousness.

The killer's hands were steady as he retrieved the nylon restraints from the pocket of his coat, a shiver of anticipation tracing the length of his spine. Moonlight filtered through the slats of the parking garage, casting angular shadows over Valerie Hudson's still form, sharpening her features. Her chest rose and fell with shallow breaths, betraying life beneath the surface of unconsciousness.

He worked methodically, looping the zip ties around her wrists with a caution bred from a blend of obsession and precision. The soft click of the fastening echoed in the hollow space, each snare a silent promise of control. With each movement, he imagined the moment she would awaken, the dawning horror in her eyes meeting his own impassive gaze. But there was no thrill in her vulnerability—no, it was the confrontation he craved, the reckoning that would come when they reached the place of her deepest despair.

Her legs were next, ankles bound with the same meticulous care, ensuring there would be no flailing, no chance for escape.

With Valerie secured, he closed the back door, the sound muffled within the confines of the car's interior. A sense of urgency now threaded through his veins, driving him forward. He slid into the driver's seat, the leather cool against his skin, the dashboard a tableau of blinking lights and dials. In this cocoon of steel and glass, he was sovereign, the arbiter of fates.

The engine's growl rose to a crescendo and then settled as he maneuvered the car with a predator's grace, headlights cutting through the darkness. The parking garage slipped away, its concrete pillars and fluorescent lights giving way to the open road. Streetlights streaked past in blurs of orange and white, the world outside reduced to a monochrome blur.

Valerie's unconscious body lay splayed across the backseat, a stark contrast to the vibrant force she embodied in the waking world. Yet here, in the quiet sanctum of his vehicle, she was merely a vessel for his purpose—a purpose etched into every fiber of his being.

Asphalt unspooled beneath them, mile after mile of relentless pursuit toward the destination that called to him—a place etched in her history that would come to define his legacy. It was there, in the crucible of her greatest trauma, that the final act would unfold. And as he drove, the city's silhouette receded, swallowed by the encroaching darkness, leaving only the road ahead—a tenebrous path leading inexorably to the endgame.

CHAPTER TWENTY THREE

Clara slid into the driver's seat, the leather cool and unwelcoming against her skin. The heavy thud of the car door shutting echoed in the stillness of the evening air, and she let out a long breath, the weight of Jack Sullivan's words lingering with her like the faint scent of cigarette smoke.

Her fingers danced across her phone's screen with practiced precision, summoning Derek Morales's contact as she started the ignition. As she pressed the phone to her ear, she glanced in the rearview mirror, catching a fleeting glimpse of her own reflection—eyes sharp with determination despite the exhaustion evidenced by the deep bags that had formed beneath them.

"Find that breakthrough yet?" Derek asked, skipping all formalities. There was a smile she could hear in his tone, and a wave of gratitude for that washed over Clara. His willingness to trust and support her process—even when that meant staying at the station doing grunt work while she went on brain breaks—was one of the reasons their partnership worked so well.

"I did," she replied, a slight smile creeping into her tone as well. "I think we've been looking at this all wrong."

There was a brief pause, and though she couldn't see him, Clara could picture Derek's brow furrowing in confusion, his mind already turning over the implications of her statement.

"Talk to me, Pike," he finally replied.

"Jack gave me a nudge in a different direction. We've been so tangled up in the victim's traumas, we've missed the forest for the trees." Her hand gripped the steering wheel tighter, the leather creaking under her hold. "We need to look for connections between the victims beyond their online past trauma. There has to be an unseen thread linking them together in the present."

"Connections?" Derek's tone shifted, a note of intrigue coloring his skepticism. "That's a broad canvas, Clara. But I'm listening."

"Exactly. It's not about what they've suffered, but whom or what they've shared in their lives. Associations we haven't considered, patterns that aren't immediately visible. It's something intangible,

Derek. We need to dig beneath the surface, analyze financials, organizations, associations—any overlap could lead us to our killer."

For a heartbeat, silence stretched between them, the anticipation tightening like a coil. Then Derek's voice sliced through the tension, decisive and focused.

"Alright, Pike. I'm with you. We'll focus in on the present instead of the past—find the common denominator now. This bastard has a connection to those women, and we're going to uncover it."

Clara felt a surge of adrenaline as she maneuvered the car back toward headquarters. The night's cloak enfolded the city, wrapping it in both darkness and possibility. Each streetlight that whizzed by painted fleeting streaks of illumination across her determined features, as if highlighting the resolve etched deeply within them.

Her mind, a restless flurry of activity, mirrored the chaos of the evening rush hour, which in DC, seemed to last well into the night. She could feel the pieces of the puzzle hovering just out of reach, like specters in a fog, waiting for her to draw them into the light. It was a feeling she knew all too well—the tantalizing proximity of truth, obscured by the shadowy veil of the unknown.

Clara pulled into the familiar confines of the FBI headquarters' parking lot, exiting her vehicle with the stealth of a predator on the prowl, her eyes scanning the perimeter, ever vigilant, ever seeking.

Inside, the building thrummed with a subdued tension, the air thick with the weight of expectation. Agents passed like ghosts, their faces etched with the strain of battles fought in the mind's silent theater. Clara navigated the sterile corridors, her shoes clicking a staccato rhythm that cut through the hush.

She found Derek in the bullpen, an island in a sea of desks, surrounded by mountains of financial records that threatened to swallow him whole. The fluorescent lights cast a pallid glow over the space, shadows dancing across his concentrated face as he sifted through the papers with systematic precision. She couldn't help but smile. His preference for physical files over digital records never ceased to baffle her, but it was just one of those things that made Derek Derek.

"Morales," Clara called out, announcing her presence.

Derek glanced up, his eyes momentarily reflecting the weariness of the long hours. Yet, there was a spark there too—a kindred spirit ignited by the chase.

"Welcome back, Pike," he said, the corner of his mouth quirking upward. "I hope you're ready to dive deep. These records are a maze, and we've got ourselves a Minotaur to find."

Clara approached, rolling up the sleeves of her blazer, her gaze locking onto the sprawl of documents. There was something almost sacred about this ritual—the preparation for the descent into the cryptic depths of data and numbers.

"Then let's begin the hunt," Clara responded, her voice steady and sure.

"Here," he sighed, handing her a manila folder. "Take the Marlowe file. I've marked some transactions that could be something—or nothing."

Clara took her seat, the chair groaning under the sudden shift. Before her lay a sprawl of documents, each a fragment of life reduced to dates and dollars. The Marlowe file bristled with tabs, neon colors attempting to impose order on chaos.

She sifted through the bank and credit card statements methodically, her fingers brushing the paper as though she could feel the imprint of intent left behind. Each withdrawal, each deposit, each purchase was a breath taken by the victim, a heartbeat now stilled. The entries blurred together, a litany of mundane purchases and routine payments, until—

"Wait," she murmured, her finger pausing mid-page. A transaction, seemingly innocuous, yet it echoed something she had seen when digging into Jessica's life the day prior. She scribbled a note on her pad—cross-referencing, always cross-referencing. Her brain churned, every tidbit of information locked in an iron grip of recall, each fact a potential key to unlocking the puzzle.

"Anything?" Derek's voice pulled her back from the precipice of thought.

"Maybe," she answered, tapping the page. "Look for this vendor in the others. It's come up more than once."

"Got it." His response was terse, his focus already tunneled back into his own search.

Together, they mined the depths of financial history, their shared determination a beacon against the encroaching dark of uncertainty. Time became fluid around them, measured only by the progress of their investigation, as they peeled back layers of the mundane in search of the sinister thread woven through the lives of the victims.

Clara's eyes were strained, the glow of the computer screen casting an otherworldly pallor on her face as she combed through another financial statement. The room was dim, save for the harsh artificial light that bore down on the scattered papers and open ledgers on the desk. The headquarters was silent at this late hour. The usual cacophony of ringing phones and murmured conversations had long since ebbed away, leaving only the soft hum of electronics and the occasional shuffling of paper to fill the void.

She leaned closer, her gaze narrowing as a name jumped out at her from the sea of transactions—a beacon in the fog. "Dr. Ian Foster," she read aloud, her voice barely above a whisper. This was the third victim who had recurring payments to his practice.

"Here too…" Her pulse quickened as she mentally consulted the other victims' files she had perused. She was certain it was there—first mentioned on pages thirteen and twenty-six respectively. A connection. Her hands began to tremble with the weight of realization. This was no coincidence; this was a pattern.

"Derek," she called out, the urgency in her voice immediately apparent.

Across the room, Derek glanced up from the mountain of paperwork he had been entrenched in. His expression was weary, lines of concentration etched deeply into his forehead. At Clara's tone, however, his fatigue seemed to evaporate, replaced by a sharp attentiveness.

"Payments to a therapist," Clara explained, moving the cursor over a website for Dr. Foster's practice. "All three made regular payments to Dr. Ian Foster."

"Could be routine therapy sessions," Derek suggested, though the skepticism in his voice belied his words.

"Maybe." Clara's response was laced with doubt. "But all of them seeing the same therapist? And one we've never heard of until now?"

Without a word, Derek turned back to his workstation, frantically flipping through the other victims' files to make sure the connection held. It took only a few minutes for him to confirm it; the connection was undeniable. Each woman had indeed been a patient of Dr. Foster's.

"Son of a—" Derek muttered under his breath, his eyes wide with the gravity of their discovery.

The silence between them was charged, the air thick with the scent of old coffee and the mustiness of worn files. They both understood the magnitude of what lay before them: a thread that linked the victims, woven into the very fabric of their lives by a therapist who was supposed to be their confidant, their healer.

Could this man, with whom they had entrusted their deepest traumas, have secretly been using their sessions as a hunting ground? The thought sent a shiver down Clara's spine. It was a cruelty almost beyond any she could imagine—though she had been in this job long enough to know there was no depth of depravity that was truly off limits for a sociopath.

She couldn't know, for sure, if Dr. Foster was this sort of man—if he was a killer disguised as a healer. But one thing was for certain: she and Derek weren't going to waste a moment before they found out.

CHAPTER TWENTY FOUR

Derek leaned back in his chair, the leather creaking under his weight as he folded his arms. His brow furrowed, a testament to the profiler's inner turmoil. "He knew their fears, their secrets. He could manipulate those traumas… turn them into blueprints for murder."

"Exactly." Clara's gaze didn't waver. She possessed an almost preternatural ability to focus on details that others would overlook, but now, it was the bigger picture that sharpened into view. "We need to confront him. Now."

The air around them grew heavy with the gravity of their decision. Despite the lateness of the hour, they both understood the urgency. Derek nodded, and they began to strategize.

"His house?" Clara suggested. "It's risky, but we can't afford to wait."

"Let's do it," Derek replied, the gears turning behind his discerning eyes. "But we go in prepared. No direct accusations. We gauge his reactions, push for an alibi."

"Agreed." Clara stood up, smoothing her jacket as she did so. Her mental gears shifted from analysis to action, the transition as swift as it was silent.

The night air was crisp as they stepped outside, the moon hanging low and casting long shadows across the parking lot. Clara felt the familiar surge of adrenaline, the kind that always preceded the pivotal moments in her career.

They made their way to the unmarked bureau SUV, the gravel crunching underfoot. As Derek slid into the driver's seat, Clara settled beside him, her thoughts aligning with the mission at hand. In the cocoon of the vehicle, the world narrowed down to just the two of them and the road that would lead them to Dr. Foster.

"Remember, we're not there to accuse, just to observe," Derek said, his hands gripping the wheel with practiced ease. "If it's okay with you, I'd like to take lead on speaking with him."

Clara glanced at him, the faint glow of the dashboard illuminating the contours of his face. "Yeah, that's fine. Gives me more time to observe," she replied. "I'll keep my eyes open. If there's something out of place, I'll notice it."

As they drove through the almost-deserted streets, the city's pulse seemed to slow, its heartbeat syncing with their own. Buildings blurred past, nondescript in the darkness, as they moved toward their destination with deliberate speed. Clara watched the scenery change, residential lights flickering like distant stars, each home a vault of secrets.

"We should be cautious," she mused aloud, breaking the silence. "Without a warrant, he could just refuse to talk to us. And us showing up this late will likely already put his hackles up."

"True," Derek agreed.

"And if he is willing to talk, that doesn't necessarily signal innocence. It could be arrogance… or a trap."

"Or confidence we won't find anything," Derek added, his voice low. "Either way, we'll find out soon enough."

The tires of the unmarked sedan whispered against the damp asphalt as Derek turned onto the tree-lined avenue where Dr. Ian Foster's home nestled among the shadows. Clara Pike's grip on the passenger armrest tightened, a silent testament to the gravity of their visit. Her eyes, sharp and discerning, scanned the elegant facades of the houses they passed, each one cloaked in the deceptive tranquility of the affluent neighborhood.

"Remember, we're not here to accuse," Derek said, his voice slicing through the tension. "We need him to talk, to slip up."

"Understood," Clara acknowledged, her thoughts a meticulous web of strategy and anticipation. "But something tells me he won't make it that easy."

A flicker of agreement passed between them, an unspoken understanding that they were venturing into the lion's den. The soft hum of the engine seemed to grow louder as they drew nearer to their destination, the sound filling the space with a sense of urgency.

Clara reached for the door handle as they neared Dr. Foster's address, her senses heightened, ready to dissect every detail of the coming encounter.

Derek eased the car to a stop in front of a stately two-story house, its facade an imposing mixture of brick and dark timber. A single lamp cast a warm glow onto the porch, piercing the darkness with an inviting beacon that belied the chilling task at hand. They exited the vehicle, their footsteps a muted symphony on the wet pavement.

As they approached the front door, Clara adjusted the badge clipped to her belt, the metal cold against her fingers. She could feel the weight of their purpose settle around them like a dense fog. Each step was calculated, a deliberate dance with the unknown.

Derek rang the bell, the sound echoing through the stillness of the night. Moments later, the door swung open, revealing Dr. Ian Foster in the flesh. He stood before them, silver hair impeccably styled, his sophisticated glasses catching the light with an academic glint. His demeanor was calm, almost unnervingly so.

"Good evening," Derek began. "I'm Special Agent Derek Morales, and this is my partner, Special Agent Clara Pike. We're with the FBI."

"Agents," Dr. Foster greeted them, his voice smooth, betraying none of the surprise one might expect at such a late hour. "What brings you to my doorstep?"

Clara met his gaze, searching for any trace of deceit. "We're sorry to disturb you, particularly so late in the evening, but we were hoping you could spare us some time, Dr. Foster," she said. "There are a few things we'd like to discuss."

"Of course," he replied, stepping aside to grant them entry. "Please, come in."

They crossed the threshold into a foyer adorned with tasteful art and rich mahogany furniture. The air was thick with the scent of old books and faint traces of sandalwood. Clara's every sense was on high alert as she took in the surroundings, knowing full well that even the smallest detail could prove essential later.

Clara studied Dr. Ian Foster as he settled into the high-backed leather chair behind his mahogany desk, an island amidst a sea of books and papers that spoke of a mind both orderly and expansive. The room was quiet except for the soft ticking of an antique clock that seemed to measure each second with deliberate gravity. Clara felt the weight of those seconds, thick with expectation and the unspoken.

"Dr. Foster," Derek began, his tone steady, his approach gentle, "I imagine you're aware that several of your patients have recently fallen prey to a serial killer who has been haunting the city. We understand the need for confidentiality in your profession, but we're dealing with multiple homicides, and we need your help."

The therapist's fingers tented before him on the desk; his eyes were steady. "I'm acutely aware of the situation, Agent Pike. But without breaching the trust of my clients—"

"Former clients," Derek interjected gently, yet firmly. "They're dead now."

"Confidentiality does not cease to apply even following the patient's death."

"I understand that," Derek offered. "But these victims—they were targeted, killed at places that we believe held traumatic significance for them. That's not the sort of thing that would have been common knowledge."

Clara watched the therapist closely. The tension in the room was palpable, like the charged air before a thunderstorm.

"Given the circumstances," Dr. Foster finally conceded, his voice softer now, resigned, "I can confirm that these women were under my care. I am bound by oath not to disclose the specifics of our sessions, but I can say that their past traumas… Well, they did relate to the locations where they met their tragic end. You're not wrong about that."

"Do you have any insight you can share that might help us find the man who is targeting them?" Derek asked.

"I don't," Dr. Foster replied, a hint of what sounded to Clara like sadness creeping into the edge of his voice. "I wish I could do more to help you, but I don't have any insight, I'm afraid. I imagine you've got a late night ahead of you, though. Can I get you some coffee before you go?"

"That would be lovely," Clara replied, both intrigued by the doctor's not-so-subtle attempt to end their interview and eager to have a moment to discuss this further with Derek.

"Just one question first. Can you provide us with an alibi for the times of the murders?" Clara asked, her gaze unwavering. "I can provide you with a list of dates and times in case you need to check your calendar."

In her peripheral vision, she saw Derek shift, ready to back her up.

"Of course." Dr. Foster gave a sigh, almost imperceptible, and Clara noted it, filing it away.

She scribbled the dates down quickly, along with the estimated times of death, and slid the piece of paper she had written them to Dr. Foster, who sighed a second time as he reviewed them.

"My wife passed a few years ago, so outside of work, my life is quite solitary these days. There's no one to vouch for my whereabouts, I'm afraid. Now, give me just a moment to go get that coffee."

He rose from his chair with the elegance of someone accustomed to being in control, and Clara listened closely to the sound of his receding footsteps, eager for him to get out of earshot.

As he left the study, Clara's mind was abuzz. Dr. Foster's alibi—or lack thereof—was troubling, yet something gnawed at her. It was too straightforward, and in her experience, the truth was rarely so accommodating. Derek met her glance, and in his eyes, she recognized a shared unease. They had a suspect, but the puzzle was far from complete.

"We have to bring him back to headquarters," Derek said, his voice low but resolute. "He's the only person who's connected to all of the victims, and he knew all of the specifics of their trauma. He needs to come in for further questioning."

Clara nodded in agreement, her mind working furiously. She couldn't shake the disquiet that clung to her like a second skin. Dr. Foster's willingness to confirm his professional relationship with the victims, his vague alibi—it was all too neatly packaged. And yet, she could sense the discordant note in the melody of his story.

"I agree," she replied, the words tasting of necessity rather than conviction. "But there's something about it that just doesn't feel right to me."

"I don't disagree," Derek replied. "But he's the only lead we've got. We have an obligation to follow it all the way through."

Before Clara could say anything else, she heard footsteps approaching the study. Dr. Foster appeared a moment later with two cups of coffee.

"Thank you," Clara said as he handed one cup to her.

"We appreciate the gesture, but I'm afraid we're going to have to take this to go," Derek said, his tone official, masking the uncertainty that Clara knew mirrored her own. "We need you to accompany us to the station for some additional questions."

"Very well," the therapist replied, his composure unflappable as if he'd anticipated this moment from the beginning.

As they drove back to the station, the city lights blurred past Clara's window, smears of yellow and red in the night. Her thoughts were a whirlwind, each one catching on the same snag—something was off. Dr. Foster's profile fit too perfectly, like a key crafted to slip smoothly into a lock it was never meant to open.

The more she analyzed things, the more the unease that had been festering within her since they first met Dr. Foster coalesced into a tangible suspicion. Her photographic memory replayed every microexpression, every inflection of the therapist's voice, searching for the missing piece. But it wasn't something she'd seen or heard that troubled her—it was an absence, a void where there should have been something substantial.

It was all too convenient, every answer Dr. Foster provided fitting into their puzzle with ease. Yet Clara's instincts screamed that the image was wrong, that they were forcing pieces together that didn't belong. The killer was still out there—she felt it in her bones. And until she could unearth the truth buried beneath layers of deception, no one was safe—not even them.

CHAPTER TWENTY FIVE

The sterile light of headquarters buzzed above, casting a pallor on Dr. Foster's silver hair as Derek's voice, steady and probing, filtered through the one-way mirror. Clara stood apart from the scene, watching from outside the room, her silhouette ghosting over the reflective surface. She couldn't shake the cold clutch of doubt that had fastened itself to her like a shadow since their interview with Dr. Foster. The pieces were there, yet they refused to fall into place, and now the itch for resolution tugged at her footsteps.

With a subtle glance at Derek, who was now leaning forward, eyes locked on the therapist's composed face, Clara turned away. She knew he had his doubts, too, and he was more than capable of handling this interrogation alone. He would understand her leaving to seek the missing link while he peeled back Foster's layers.

For a moment, she considered telling him where she was going, but she didn't want to risk interrupting his interrogative flow. So, instead, she made the decision to just leave, trusting that he knew her well enough to both know and understand her impulse to investigate further.

Her boots met the linoleum floor in a rhythmic testament to her resolve as she exited the building, the cool air outside offering a sharp contrast to the stifled atmosphere she'd left behind.

Clara walked with purpose through the city, her gaze flickering across faces and storefronts. The familiar weight of her badge against her chest was a silent reminder of the stakes at play. Somewhere within this urban labyrinth lurked a predator masked by anonymity, a hunter of the scarred and broken. If she was right, and Dr. Foster wasn't their unsub, then what was his connection? How did the killer know about each victim's prior traumas, if not through their therapy sessions?

The question gnawed at the edges of her consciousness, refusing to be stilled. Each step echoed the relentless drum of her own thoughts, a beat urging her onward. Clara felt the city's heartbeat beneath her feet, the thrum of life that held both promise and peril.

She pressed on, her senses attuned to every shift in the wind, every whispered conversation that skittered past her ears. There was a rhythm to the chaos, a pattern that teased the fringes of her perception.

Clara navigated the labyrinthine alleys that ran like veins behind the city's façade. Her boots, scuffed from miles of pursuit, tapped a staccato rhythm against the damp cobblestones, articulating her inner turmoil. The chill in the air was biting, gnawing through her leather jacket as if it were paper, but it was the unsolved puzzle that truly set her teeth on edge. How did the killer know?

Beneath the intermittent glow of flickering street lamps, she replayed each case in her mind, scrutinizing the invisible thread woven through the tragic tapestry of the victims' lives. Cassie Marlowe, Jessica Hanley, Naomi Watson, and Lila Torres—women linked by their silent screams and a killer who seemed to whisper into the void of their deepest fears. Dr. Foster, with his sympathetic nods and practiced concern, should have been the vessel of their secrets, yet intuition pricked at Clara, insisting that the answer lay elsewhere.

Her gaze swept across the darkened windows of closed shops, reflections of a city too preoccupied to notice its own darkness. It was in this quiet hour, when the hum of urban existence had ebbed, that clarity often visited her. She paused, allowing the silence to envelop her. And then, like a camera lens snapping into focus, an image crystallized in her mind: microphones, devices hidden within the sanctity of a confessional haven. A bugged office.

The thought sent a jolt through her. Could someone have infiltrated Dr. Foster's space, feasting on the vulnerabilities laid bare within those walls? If so, the implications were monstrous, the breach of trust unthinkable. But it made sense; it would explain how the killer moved with such precision, striking at the core of each woman's pain.

Adrenaline surged through her veins as she considered the possibility. If her hunch was right, the key to unraveling this enigma wasn't buried in the past—it was planted in the here and now, listening, recording, waiting. It was a chilling prospect, one that conjured images of a predator silently stalking its prey.

Clara Pike's fingers danced over her phone, the glowing screen a beacon in the murky midnight. Her mind was a whir of cogs and gears, clicking into place with every step she took along the dampened sidewalks. Night had draped its dark veil over the city, the streetlights casting long shadows that slithered across the concrete like sinister serpents. The ambient hum of the city's nightlife pulsed around her, but Clara was deaf to it all—her focus singular, her goal clear.

She pressed the call button, and the line buzzed in her ear, a modern-day oracle waiting to be consulted. Derek answered on the third ring, his voice a blend of fatigue and latent curiosity.

"Clara? What's going on?"

"Are you still with Foster?" she asked, her query slicing through pleasantries like a scalpel.

"Interrogation just wrapped up. He's in holding now, but we're getting nowhere fast," Derek replied, a tinge of frustration lacing his words. "You got something?"

"Possibly," she said, pausing as she reached the corner of the block, the neon sign of a nearby bar flickering irregularly. "I need you to convince him to let us into his office tonight."

"Tonight? Clara, what are you thinking?"

"Think about it, Derek. How could the killer know intimate details without being the therapist himself?" she posited, her breath visible in the cold air as she spoke. "If I'm right, and it's not Dr. Foster, then the most obvious answer is that his office must be bugged."

A silence fell between them for a heartbeat too long, and Clara knew the wheels were turning in Derek's head.

"Okay, say there's some merit to this theory," he conceded at last. "Patient confidentiality is a minefield. Foster won't give permission easily."

"Tell him we won't look at the files. We just need access to the physical space," Clara pressed, her gaze scanning the desolate alleyway beside her, half-expecting to catch a glint of a hidden lens or microphone. "Look, we could always get a warrant, but that's going to take forever, and with the way the killer is accelerating, there's a good chance that's time we don't have."

"I know, but—"

"If we find something, it could prove his innocence. It's in his best interest to let me in."

"That may be true, but—"

"Come on, Derek. You're the most persuasive person I know. At least try?" Clara asked.

"Alright," Derek sighed, the sound crackling over the connection. "Let me see what I can do."

The line went dead, and Clara tucked the phone back into her coat pocket, the fabric brushing against the concealed badge that marked her purpose. She felt the weight of the night closing in, the darkness almost palpable. Every fiber of her being was taut with anticipation, the hunter within scenting a trail.

Minutes stretched into an eternity until her phone vibrated, jolting her back to the present. Derek's name flashed across the screen, and she answered with a briskness born of urgency.

"Got it," he said, his words crisp and short. "Foster's agreeing to let you go in. He's rattled, thinks it might clear his name. But he's adamant, Clara. You absolutely cannot do anything other than check for bugs. No matter how tempting, you cannot look at any of the files. Even if it could help break the case."

"I understand," she responded, her voice low, a mix of relief and determination threading through her. "I'm heading there now."

"Be careful, Clara," Derek cautioned, but she had already ended the call, her steps quickening as she moved with the stealth of a shadow toward her destination.

Dr. Foster's office building stood unassuming, its facade betraying nothing of the potential horrors it might house within. Clara took a breath and steadied herself before brandishing a small lock-picking kit from her purse and getting to work.

The lock surrendered with a soft click, almost imperceptible in the stillness of the corridor. Clara Pike's hands, adept and nimble, stilled for a moment as she listened intently for any sign of movement within Dr. Foster's office. Silence, thick and expectant, hung in the air, save for the distant hum of the city that never truly slept. She pushed the door open with the caution of one who understood that even empty rooms could harbor unseen threats.

As she crossed the threshold, the eerie stillness of the deserted reception area greeted her. This was it—the sanctum where the wounded came seeking solace, unaware of the invisible specter that may have preyed upon their confessions. She made her way to the doctor's office and once again began working on the lock. This one gave way even quicker, and she stepped into the office with a sense of both urgency and respect.

Inside, shadows clung to the corners like cobwebs, undisturbed by the intrusion. The office was a tableau of muted colors and soft furnishings designed to put the mind at ease, yet now it stood testament to an unsettling possibility. Clara's eyes, sharp and searching, swept across the room, taking in the lay of the land before venturing further into its depths. She made her way to the therapist's desk, a polished expanse of cherrywood.

With methodical precision, she began her search. Every sweep of her hands was deliberate, every breath measured, as she searched for the malignant whisper of technology where it had no right to be.

Thankfully, it wasn't long before her fingers brushed against something foreign—a small, nearly imperceptible irregularity beneath the edge of the desk. A bug, sophisticated enough to go unnoticed by those untrained to look for such treachery. The revelation hit her with a cold certainty: someone had turned this place of healing into a den of espionage.

Clara wasted no time pulling out her phone and calling Derek.

"Morales," Derek answered on the second ring, his voice betraying a hint of apprehension that matched the hour.

"I was right. His office was bugged," Clara said without preamble, the words uncoiling like smoke into the night. "We've been chasing our tails, Derek. The killer is smarter than we gave them credit for."

There was a beat of silence on the other end, the kind that spoke volumes of Derek's own realizations dawning in the dim light of their discovery.

"Damn it," he finally muttered, the profiler in him piecing together the implications. "I should have seen that. Foster didn't fit the profile, and this—it's the only way they could've known about the victims' traumas so intimately. They were listening, learning… calculating."

"No point in playing 'woulda coulda shoulda,'" Clara said. "We know now. Now, the question is, what do we do with that knowledge?"

"Foster would have kept access to that room really limited," Derek mused. "Maybe a cleaner here or there, but mostly, the only people who would have access are—"

"His patients," Clara interjected, her gaze fixed on the malignant piece of metal now lying innocuous on the desk.

"Though I can't imagine he would have left them alone in there much either."

"No," Clara replied. "But it only takes a second to plant a bug. If Foster had to use the bathroom, or was distracted—"

"Alright," Derek replied, his tone shifting from surprise to steely resolve. "I'll see if Foster will part with a list of his patients. See if anything sticks out. In the meantime, don't touch anything else. We'll need to get a team to sweep the entire office."

"Understood," Clara acknowledged, though her eyes remained locked on the device that had so callously invaded the sanctum of trust between doctor and patient. She wasn't one to sit back; action pulsed through her veins. But for now, she would let the system work its course.

"In the meantime," Clara said, "can you get Foster out of holding and into interrogation? I'd like to speak with him."

"Of course," Derek replied.

"Great. I'll be back in just a few."

With that, Clara raced out of the office and back to headquarters, eager to get in the box with Foster—to see what answers, if any, he could offer to help her finally break the case.

Clara made it back to headquarters in record time, and in a matter of minutes was standing in the sterile interrogation room, the buzz of fluorescent lights overhead blending with the hum of tension in the air. Dr. Ian Foster sat across from her. His hands, clasped together on the table, were steady, betraying no sign of nervousness.

"Dr. Foster," Clara began, her voice calm but authoritative, "I appreciate you letting me access your office. That was a tremendous help."

"I'm glad," he replied, and though he seemed sincere, Clara could not help but note a hint of leeriness in his voice.

"And now, I'm afraid I need to ask for your help one more time. We need to talk about your patients."

"Agent Pike," he replied, his tone, for the first time, edged with genuine irritation, "we've been over this. My patients' confidentiality is sacrosanct. I cannot simply hand over their private information without due process."

"Understood." She nodded. "But we're talking about a serial killer who knows intimate details about the victims—details he got by bugging your office."

Dr. Foster's expression remained impassive, his gaze unwavering as he met her eyes. "And I feel awful about that. It is a betrayal of the highest magnitude. But I assure you, Agent Pike, none of my clients are capable of such atrocities. And without a subpoena, my hands are tied."

Clara felt the frustration gnaw at her but pushed it aside. She needed to remain focused, to think outside the box. The tight space of the room seemed to close in around her, the stark white walls a blank canvas for her thoughts.

"Okay, let's approach this differently," Clara said, her mind racing as another angle presented itself. She closed her eyes for a moment, allowing her photographic memory to conjure up the images from Oliver Belmont's gallery. Almost instantaneously, each photograph appeared before her, crisp and clear, as if she were standing right in front of them.

"Dr. Foster," she continued, opening her eyes to find him watching her curiously, "there was a photograph at Naomi's crime scene. One that seemed to be connected to a collection of photographs at a local art gallery that had pictures of various places around the city. At least one of those other crime scenes was represented in those photographs."

He raised an eyebrow, intrigued despite himself. "Go on."

"We dismissed it as a lead because there was no obvious connection to Jessica Hanley's crime scene or the gym where Lila Torres was killed, but in retrospect, I'm beginning to wonder if that was true. Perhaps the gym where Lila worked wasn't always a gym. Maybe it was something else first—something that would have been featured in those photographs."

"Okay..." Dr. Foster offered, clearly interested but also unsure precisely where Clara was going with this. To be fair, Clara wasn't yet entirely sure herself.

"We thought the killer was just picking locations based on the site of the victims' trauma, but what if that's wrong? What if he's picking the victims based on the locations of their trauma and the connection of those locations to these photographs, even if what is at the locations is different now? So in that case, the photos could still be relevant. With that in mind..."

Dr. Foster's demeanor shifted subtly; the notion had hit a nerve. "You believe these photographs are significant?"

"Perhaps." Clara leaned forward, her gaze intense. "If you're not comfortable implicating any of your patients in a crime without concrete proof, okay. But maybe we can work backwards. Maybe you can help me identify his next victim. Surely you can't object to using your knowledge of your patients to save a life? Isn't that the basis of the Hippocratic oath?"

Dr. Foster considered this quietly for a moment, and with each passing second, Clara felt the tension tighten around her throat. She needed answers, and she needed them now. And while she respected Dr. Foster's ethics, she couldn't afford to let that slow them down. Not when a life was on the line.

"Alright," he answered finally. "What do you need me to do?"

Clara closed her eyes and once again pulled up all of the photos in the gallery in her mind's eye.

"There's an old school," she began. "Red brick with white accents. It has thirty-six Palladian windows and two arched doorways with black handrails leading up to them. There are four brick pillars out front, one next to each door and one on each side of the building. There are spires on the roof and two trees against the wall. One cyprus cedar, one sycamore."

She continued on like this, describing each building, each location, to the doctor, who watched her with a mixture of fascination and anxiety.

When she finished, she opened her eyes and looked at him pleadingly.

"What do you think, Doctor? Is there a chance any of your patients might have a connection to these places? A traumatic event that occurred there, something they discussed during therapy?"

For a moment, silence filled the room as Dr. Foster considered her question. Clara watched him closely, searching for any flicker of realization, any sign that this new lead might bear fruit.

"Dr. Foster," Clara urged, her voice a low, steady drumbeat against the tense silence of the room, "think. Please, this is important."

Dr. Foster's face was a mask of concentration, the gears of his mind almost visibly turning behind furrowed brows. And then, something shifted in his expression, and Clara knew they had hit pay dirt. "Yes," he breathed, almost reluctantly. "There is someone."

"Who?" Clara leaned in, her pulse quickening.

"Valerie Hudson," Dr. Foster said quietly. "She was assaulted at the courthouse a few years ago. It was a particularly brutal case."

Clara felt a chill slither down her spine.

"Tell me about her," Clara prompted, her mind already piecing together the harrowing story that Valerie must have lived through.

"Valerie is—was—a brilliant lawyer," Dr. Foster began, his voice tinged with a respect that transcended the patient-doctor confidentiality he held so dear. "She came to me after the assault, struggling with the trauma. It happened right before the biggest case of her life. The courthouse was supposed to be her battlefield, not the site of her own personal hell."

A sense of dread settled over Clara. The pieces were falling into place, forming a picture that was as clear as it was horrifying. Valerie Hudson had to be the next victim, her narrative soon to be brutally ended in the very place where she had once fought for truth.

"I tried my best to help her. I'm still trying. But she was never able to step back into the courtroom after that. She had to leave the practice of law altogether."

"Thank you, Dr. Foster," Clara said softly. "You may have just saved Valerie Hudson's life."

Clara stepped out of the room, her mind ablaze with determination. The hunt was narrowing, the shadows drawing back to reveal a killer hiding in plain sight. Valerie Hudson's story would not have the same tragic end the other women's had; Clara would see to that. With a grim set to her jaw, she made her way to Derek. They had a new lead, and time was of the essence.

CHAPTER TWENTY SIX

Clara Pike's footsteps echoed on the concrete as she made her way out of FBI headquarters and into the enormous parking lot. The city's breaths came in short, cold gusts, ruffling her hair and nipping at the exposed skin of her neck. She reached into the depths of her coat pocket, retrieving her phone with a sense of urgency that mirrored the chaotic rhythm of her heart. Without breaking stride, she dialed Valerie Hudson's number.

"Come on, Valerie," she muttered, willing the call to connect.

But it was to no avail. The impersonal voicemail greeting was like a sledgehammer to Clara's heightened instincts. She could feel it in her bones. Something was terribly wrong. Clara cut the call short, the silence left behind by the unresponsive line echoing ominously in her ears.

"Damn it," she hissed under her breath.

"Voicemail?" Derek stood a few paces away, his keen eyes studying Clara's expression, which was etched with concern.

"Directly." Clara's voice was taut as a drawn bowstring, her mind racing through countless scenarios, each more sinister than the last.

"Let's trace her phone," Derek suggested, his own voice betraying an edge of urgency. Together, they moved to the relative privacy of a nearby alleyway, shielded from prying eyes. With efficient movements born of too many similar situations, Derek pulled out his government-issued device and began the process known only to those with federal clearance.

Minutes ticked by, each one heavy with silent tension until the device emitted a low, negative beep. "It's off," Derek confirmed, his jaw setting firmly, the profiler in him already drawing conclusions.

"Or destroyed," Clara added darkly, her eyes narrowing as she processed this new piece of information. The courthouse flashed into her mind's eye—the place where Valerie's world had once come crashing down, and now potentially the stage for a final, deadly act.

"If he's got her, he's taking her to the courthouse. We need to go there now," Clara said, her voice leaving no room for argument.

Derek nodded once, his professional veneer concealing the turmoil within. "Agreed."

They exchanged a look of mutual understanding. No words were necessary; their partnership had long since transcended verbal communication. Each knew the stakes, understood the silent language of tight lips and furrowed brows. And so, without another word, they set off toward the car, their strides purposeful, driven by the knowledge that time—and a killer—waited for no one.

The engine of the black SUV roared to life, a beast awakened in the heart of the city's labyrinthine streets. Clara's fingers gripped the handle above her door—a lifeline—as they sped toward the courthouse, sirens silent to avoid announcing their approach. The moonlight bled through the cityscape, casting elongated shadows that danced across Derek's focused expression. Every turn, every acceleration was a step closer to a confrontation with a killer who had eluded them for far too long.

Clara's mind, ever precise and calculating, ran through the dossier of Valerie Hudson. Her visage flashed behind Clara's eyelids each time she blinked. She imagined Valerie in the courthouse, a hand poised just above her, ready to steal away yet another life unjustly condemned by the killer's twisted sense of retribution. Valerie's sharp features, her perseverance, flickered at the edges of Clara's consciousness, fueling the urgency pulsing through her veins.

They screeched to a halt outside the courthouse. The neoclassical architecture, usually a symbol of justice and order, now stood as a foreboding monolith under the cloak of night. They exited the vehicle, Derek leading as they breached the courthouse's steps—two specters gliding through the gloom.

Inside, the sprawling corridors were eerily hushed, the day's legal battles having retreated into the silence of nightfall. The marble floors, echoing earlier that day with the footsteps of the just and the condemned alike, now bore witness to only their stealthy tread.

Then she saw it—the subtle displacement of air, a faint tremor in the stillness ahead. Her pulse quickened, instincts honed by years of navigating the fine line between hunter and hunted. With a gesture to Derek, they veered left, moving with a predator's grace toward the disturbance.

As they approached, the figure became discernible, propped against the wall with an unnatural rigidity. It was Valerie, her form silhouetted by the scant moonlight filtering through the high windows. The sight sent a shockwave through Clara's system, but her training quelled the surge of emotion, funneling it into focus.

Valerie's chest rose and fell with shallow, ragged breaths that seemed to claw their way out from behind the gag stifling her cries. Clara could see the veins in Valerie's neck straining against her skin, a testament to the desperate struggle for sound, for air, for life. The lawyer's eyes, wide and glistening with the sheen of terror, met Clara's for a fleeting moment. They were pools of silent pleading, each blink a Morse code of distress.

The killer stood over Valerie, his posture relaxed yet predatory, like a wolf savoring the fear of its cornered prey. The knife in his hand caught a flash of light as he tilted it, inspecting the blade with an artisan's eye. His gaze was locked onto Valerie, ensuring she was acutely aware of the sharp promise of pain hovering mere inches from her.

Clara knew this tableau was the killer's masterpiece, the culmination of his twisted need to make others confront their suffering, though she'd not yet learned enough about him to know why. What she did know, however, was that this time, she would not allow him to dictate the narrative.

With each sinew in her body coiled tight, Clara launched herself toward the killer. Her movements were a blend of honed instinct and meticulous training, a dance with danger she had rehearsed countless times in her mind. The distance between them evaporated under the urgency of her sprint, her focus narrowing to the glint of the knife and the man who wielded it.

As she neared, the man's head snapped up, his features twisting into a snarl of surprise and rage. The killer adjusted his stance, preparing to meet Clara's assault. She could see the calculation in his eyes, the rapid reassessment of his plan now that his control was slipping. But Clara was already airborne, her body a projectile aimed at disarming and disabling.

She collided with the killer with the full force of her momentum, the impact jolting through her frame as they tumbled to the ground. Somehow the killer held onto the knife, which sang a high-pitched tune of metal against stone as the hand with the blade hit the floor. For a moment, time seemed elastic, stretching thin between the beats of Clara's heart as she grappled with the man beneath her.

Valerie's muffled gasps filled the air, a soundtrack to the struggle as Clara fought to keep the killer pinned. She could feel his muscles tensing beneath her, ready to throw her off, to regain the upper hand. But Clara was relentless, her determination fueled by the fierce desire to save Valerie from becoming another ghost that haunted her.

The killer bucked beneath her, but Clara shifted her weight, using his own motions against him. Her training melded with raw survival instinct, each motion purposeful, each breath a silent oath to bring this killer to justice.

She heard Derek yell for the killer to stop. She heard him identify them as FBI agents, but that didn't stop him. If anything, it only made the killer struggle harder. Clara knew Derek's instincts would be to join the fray, but that wasn't where she needed him right now. She needed him to focus on the victim—to get her out of here before she suffered any more undue trauma.

"Get Valerie," Clara managed to choke out.

She knew Derek would be reluctant, but she also knew he trusted her. And he'd seen her in enough scrapes to know that she rarely got herself into an altercation that she could not get herself out of.

The killer's breath was hot and erratic against Clara's cheek as they wrestled on the cool marble floor of the courthouse. Every muscle in her body strained, her fingers grappling for a hold on his wrist to keep the glinting knife at bay. Her mind, usually a vault of razor-sharp recollections, now narrowed to a singular focus: survival. The struggle was a macabre dance atop the intricate mosaic tiles that told a story of justice in their design—justice she was fighting to deliver.

Suddenly, the killer's strength surged. His twisted face loomed over Clara with malevolent intent, the blade inching perilously close to her jugular. Clara's heart hammered against her ribs, each beat a deafening drum in the silence of the courthouse. She could visualize every detail of the weapon, its lethal sharpness promising an end as final as the gavel's fall. Maybe having Derek focus on Valerie hadn't been the right move after all.

"Clara!" The voice cut through the tension like the very knife threatening her life. Almost instantaneously, Derek's presence filled the space, his silhouette an anchor in the tempest. With a swift motion born of years of honed instinct, he seized the killer's arm, wrenching it back with a force that echoed through the chamber. The killer's grip on the knife faltered, and the weapon clattered to the ground, sliding away on the polished surface until it came to rest near the base of Lady Justice's blindfolded statue.

As Derek fought to subdue the killer, Clara scrambled to her feet. Her limbs trembled with adrenaline, but her resolve never wavered. She grabbed the knife, ensuring that the killer could not access it no matter what happened in the confrontation with Derek, and then rushed to Valerie's side, where the lawyer sat bound and gagged, her eyes wide with the terror of her ordeal. Kneeling beside her, Clara worked quickly to untie the knots that imprisoned Valerie's feet, her fingers deft and sure despite the lingering tremors.

"Valerie, you're going to be okay," Clara whispered, her voice a soft promise in the midst of chaos. She peeled away the gag, offering a smile that held both reassurance and a shared understanding of the horrors they had faced. "We've got you."

Valerie's breath hitched with a sob as Clara helped her to stand, steadying her with a firm grip. Together, they moved away from the scene unfolding behind them—Derek's authoritative commands intermingling with the killer's snarls of defiance as he was placed in handcuffs. Clara felt the weight of Valerie's reliance on her, a burden she bore willingly. In this moment, she was not just an agent; she was a beacon of hope amid the shadows of fear.

Guiding Valerie to safety, Clara cast a glance back at Derek, who had the killer pressed face-down on the floor, his arms secured behind him. As the sirens wailed in the distance, growing ever closer, Clara knew that the night's darkness would lift, yielding to the dawn of justice. And with it, perhaps, a measure of peace for the ghosts that haunted her.

EPILOGUE

Clara's consciousness fought against the thick shroud of sleep, a losing battle until the insistent vibration of her phone on the nightstand drilled through her dreams. She lurched upright, heart pounding in the darkened room, her hand fumbling for the device. The screen blazed to life, casting long shadows across the disheveled sheets as she squinted at the message blinking there: "Director Shaw. ASAP."

The text was like ice water to her foggy brain, and exhaustion receded, replaced by a familiar surge of adrenaline.

She swung her legs over the side of the bed, feet meeting the cold floor. She padded to the kitchen, flicking on lights as she went, chasing away the shadows that lingered like unwanted thoughts. The coffee maker sputtered to life at her touch, a rich aroma soon permeating the stillness of her apartment.

With the warmth of the mug seeping into her hands, Clara allowed herself a moment to stare out the window into the early stages of dawn.

Shaking off the creeping chill, Clara donned her jacket, the fabric settling over her shoulders like armor. Her badge and gun, always within reach, found their places on her belt with practiced ease. She took one last glance around her apartment, the walls lined with notes and photos—remnants of cases past and present—before stepping out into the brisk morning air, where the sun had yet to claim the sky from the retreating night.

Her car sat amongst several others in the lot, frosted windows reflecting the faint glow of the rising sun. As she scraped away the ice, her breath hung in the air, a fleeting testament to her presence in an otherwise silent world. The engine roared to life, a steady thrum beneath her fingertips as she steered toward the looming silhouette of the FBI headquarters.

The building rose up before her, a monolith of glass and steel that held within its walls the weight of justice and the burden of truth. Clara parked and entered, the familiar buzz of fluorescent lighting greeting her. Agents and analysts moved about, their faces set in determination or fatigue—it was often hard to tell which. She navigated the labyrinthine hallways with purpose, her mind already shifting gears to whatever awaited her behind Director Shaw's door.

As she approached, her pulse quickening, she replayed the events that led them here: the courthouse, the killer's twisted plan, Valerie's near-death experience. The case may have been closed, but the aftermath was never clean, never simple.

Clara's boots clicked against the polished floor, each step a sharp echo in the corridor. The walls, adorned with commendations and somber portraits of past directors, seemed to scrutinize her as she approached Director Shaw's office. She paused, straightening her jacket—a subconscious effort to steel herself. When Derek joined her, his presence was both a comfort and a reminder of the gravity that lay beyond the frosted glass door.

"Ready?" Derek's voice was a low rumble, his dark eyes mirroring the tension in her own.

"Let's do this," Clara replied, her hand reaching for the handle.

The air inside Shaw's office was thick with the scent of mahogany and leather—trappings of authority that had always felt alien to Clara. Evelyn Shaw stood behind her desk with the poise of someone who had weathered countless storms. Her gaze, piercing and evaluating, settled on them as they entered, conveying silent appreciation.

"Agents Pike and Morales," Director Shaw began, her tone betraying a hint of warmth. "Take a seat."

They complied, the leather chairs creaking under their weight.

"The man you arrested last night, Adrian Hale, has confessed," Shaw announced, her words slicing through the tension. "To everything—all four murders. Thanks to your tenacity, he's behind bars, and with his confession, he's going to stay there." Shaw's lips curved into a semblance of a smile—a sight Clara almost wouldn't have believed if she hadn't seen it. "You've done excellent work on this case."

The praise hung heavy in the air, mingling with the unspoken acknowledgment of the lives lost—lives they hadn't been able to save.

"Thank you, ma'am," Clara replied. Atta-girls were rare in this business, especially from Director Shaw, and she knew better than to ignore that kindness.

Shaw leaned forward, her hands clasping the edge of the desk. "I know this hasn't been easy on either of you," she said, her voice softening. "But you've stopped a monster. You should take pride in that."

"Is there anything else we need to know about Hale's confession?" Derek asked, his analytical mind ever probing.

"Everything will be in the debriefing report," Shaw replied. "Though you might want to take a close look at the section on his childhood. It'll definitely fill in some gaps for you."

Clara looked at her curiously. Shaw correctly read that as a desire for more information and continued.

"Hale's father was an abusive son of a bitch. Mother just took it until the kid was ten. Then she killed herself, leaving him alone with that monster. He blamed her and her unwillingness to confront her trauma for everything that came after."

"Makes sense," Derek said.

"You should also take a look at the picture of his mother. Woman's the spitting image of Valerie Hudson. But you can look into all of that later. For right now, I want you both to take some time. Decompress. You've earned it."

"Understood, ma'am," Derek acknowledged, a shadow crossing his features momentarily before he masked it with stoic professionalism.

Clara simply nodded, her mind already wandering to the next horizon, to the unanswered questions that lay dormant within her, like coals waiting to be stoked into flame.

The heavy door of Director Shaw's office clicked shut behind Clara and Derek, sealing away the formalities and the stifling air of bureaucracy. Derek's gaze met Clara's, a silent conversation passing between them. Relief mingled with an undercurrent of weariness—a weariness that spoke of sleepless nights and relentless days.

"Hey," Derek began, his voice low, "you did good."

Clara's lips twitched in an approximation of a smile, her eyes betraying the fatigue she felt deep in her bones. The adrenaline that had fueled her through the courthouse chase had long since ebbed away, leaving a dull ache in its place.

"Thanks," she murmured, shifting her weight from one foot to the other. Her suit felt too tight, the fabric sticking to her skin in places she dared not adjust in the open corridor. "You too."

Derek leaned against the wall, his jacket creasing with the movement. "We should celebrate. I know this great place—"

"Can't," Clara interjected before he could finish. Her voice was gentle but firm, her resolve palpable. "There's something I need to do first."

"Something more important than a victory meal?" Derek's eyebrows lifted in mock incredulity, though his eyes held understanding. He knew her well enough to recognize the signs, the subtle shifts in her demeanor when she was onto something—or when something was gnawing at her.

"Yeah," she admitted, her gaze drifting past him as if she could see through the walls and into the distance beyond. The fluorescent light above flickered, casting a momentarily harsh glare over her features. Clara blinked away the intrusion, refocusing on Derek. "I just… I need some time alone. To think."

"Alright," he conceded, pushing off from the wall. "Just promise me you won't go diving into another case. You need rest, Pike."

"Promise," she lied smoothly, or at least tried to. Clara knew that Derek could read the unspoken intent behind her words as clearly as if she had broadcast it aloud.

"Take care of yourself, Clara," he said, concern lacing his tone. He hesitated for a moment, as if contemplating whether to say more, then seemed to think better of it.

"Always do," she replied, forcing a smile as she turned away from him and strode down the hallway.

***

Clara's hands gripped the steering wheel, the leather cool and pliant beneath her fingers. The road to her parents' house was familiar in a haunting, distant way, like a song remembered from childhood. She drove through the suburban streets with minimal conscious thought, relying on muscle memory and instinct honed by years of investigative work. Trees lined the route—their branches gnarled and skeletal against the slate-gray sky, casting long shadows that seemed to reach out for her passing car. The sun had begun its ascent, painting the horizon in hues of orange and mauve, but the colors held no warmth, merely specters of the approaching day.

As she neared her destination, the houses grew larger and more imposing. Clara's heart rate ticked up a notch, the thrumming in her chest a counterpoint to the steady hum of the engine. These were the streets of her youth, the backdrop to memories both cherished and painful. Her photographic memory did not allow her the luxury of forgetting, and every crack in the sidewalk, every weathered mailbox, was an archive of the past.

She pulled into the driveway of her childhood home, the quiet splintering as gravel crunched under the tires. It had been years since she last visited, and yet nothing seemed to have changed. The two-story colonial house stood proud and unyielding, its white paint pristine, the shutters still that same calming shade of blue. Clara cut the engine, the silence amplifying the pounding in her chest. Taking a deep breath, she stepped out of the car.

The air was crisp, carrying the promise of frost, and Clara wrapped her jacket tighter around herself as she approached the front door. Each step felt momentous, narrowing the distance between present and past, between the FBI agent she had become and the girl who had left all this behind.

Clara raised her hand and knocked. The sound echoed, a hollow declaration of her arrival. Time stretched, taut and expectant, and for an instant, she wondered if she should have called ahead. But the door swung open, dispelling her doubts.

Her mother stood there, a figure framed in the narrow doorway. She was older now, lines etched into her face like delicate script, telling tales of years filled with joy and sorrow. Her eyes, wide and oceanic, held a depth of emotion that belied her poised exterior.

"Clara," her mother breathed, the name a whisper that seemed to hang in the air between them. There was shock there, certainly, but something else too—a flicker of hope that Clara could not quite define.

"Mom," Clara replied, her voice steadier than she felt. Her mother seemed frozen, as if unsure of how to bridge the gulf of time and silence that lay between them.

"Come in, dear," her mother finally said, stepping aside and gesturing for Clara to enter.

As Clara crossed the threshold, the smell of the house enveloped her—the faint scent of lavender and the underlying richness of old wood. It was a scent that spoke of stability and safety, concepts that had become foreign to Clara in her line of work. She stepped inside, her resolve solidifying with each stride. This was where it all began, and somehow, Clara knew this was where she would find the strength for what needed to be done next.

Clara perched on the edge of the sofa, its floral pattern faded with time, as if it had been trying to recede into the background along with her family's unspoken woes. Her mother sat across from her, two cups of tea cradled on the coffee table between them, steam curling up like wistful spirits. The room was still, save for the rhythmic tick of the grandfather clock—an omnipresent observer marking the moments of confrontation and reconciliation.

"Mom," Clara began, her voice cutting through the silence with the precision of a detective dissecting a case. "We never really talked about…about what happened to Jake. It's like we buried it with him."

Her mother's eyes flickered with a sorrow that seemed to echo off the walls, filling the space with the weight of years of suppressed grief. "I know," she said, her voice trembling like a leaf caught in an uncertain breeze. "After your brother...after we lost him, I didn't know how to face it. How to face you."

Clara felt a familiar ache bloom within her chest, a thorned vine wrapping around her heart. She remembered the nights spent poring over the scant details of her brother's unsolved murder, the way the images had seared themselves into her photographic memory, refusing to fade or be forgotten. "It changed everything," Clara admitted. "I couldn't stay here, surrounded by memories I couldn't piece together. I thought if I could just solve cases, make sense of other people's chaos..."

"You hoped it would fill the void," her mother finished for her, a tear tracing a silent path down her cheek.

Clara nodded, her own eyes stinging with the threat of tears. She had indeed sought solace in the order and resolution of closed cases, but the specter of her brother's unsolved murder lingered, always just out of reach, a puzzle missing its final piece.

"And you and Dad..." she continued, though she didn't know quite what to say. But then the words came.

They spoke for hours, each finally sharing the unveiled truths they'd hidden from each other for so long. It was healing and something they'd badly needed, but Clara knew there was something they all needed more. Closure.

As the conversation waned and the scent of lavender grew more distant, Clara rose from the couch. The house creaked softly under her steps as she moved toward the door. Her hand paused on the doorknob, cool metal grounding her resolve.

"Mom," Clara said, turning back to face her mother. "I'm going to reopen Jake's case. I need to find out who killed him. We deserve that much."

The words hung in the air, a declaration of intent that broke the spell of the past. There was a pause. Clara could tell her mother wanted to say something in response, but she couldn't find the words. So, instead, she simply said, "Drive safe, honey. Let me know when you've made it back home."

Clara nodded and then stepped out into the cloudy afternoon, the door closing behind her with a quiet click that seemed to resonate with finality. In her mind's eye, she saw her brother's file—the one she'd been too scared to look at again all these years. She saw the photos, the evidence—all laid out in meticulous detail, awaiting her undivided attention.

As she walked to her car, the sky overhead brooded with the promise of a storm, clouds knitting together in a darkening tapestry. Clara slid into the driver's seat, hands gripping the steering wheel with renewed purpose. She would retrace the steps, reexamine the clues, and this time, she would not rest until the truth was unearthed. After all, she was Clara Pike, and her memory—her greatest weapon—would not fail her now. With the engine coming to life beneath her, she whispered a vow into the gathering darkness: "I'm going to do it, Jake. I'm going to find you justice."

NOW AVAILABLE!

REMEMBER THE DEAD
(A Clara Pike FBI Thriller—Book Two)

When victims connected to a controversial drug trial fall prey to a vengeful killer, FBI Agent Clara Pike must use her exceptional memory to solve the crimes. With each detail seared into her mind, Clara embarks on a high-stakes hunt for justice—but can she uncover the truth before more victims are lost?

"Molly Black has written a taut thriller that will keep you on the edge of your seat… I absolutely loved this book and can't wait to read the next book in the series!"
—Reader review for Girl One: Murder

REMEMBER THE DEAD is book #2 in a long anticipated new series by critically-acclaimed and #1 bestselling mystery and suspense author Molly Black, whose books have received over 2,000 five-star reviews and ratings. The series begins with REMEMBER THE FEAR (Book #1).

The Clara Pike series is an electrifying and intense crime thriller that follows a gifted yet troubled female protagonist. This compelling narrative is a whirlwind of relentless action, gripping suspense, unexpected twists, and eye-opening surprises, with a fast-paced rhythm that will keep you turning pages well into the night. Fans of Rachel Caine, Karin Slaughter, and Teresa Driscoll are sure to fall in love.

Future books in the series will be available soon.

"I binge read this book. It hooked me in and didn't stop till the last few pages… I look forward to reading more!"
—Reader review for Found You

"I loved this book! Fast-paced plot, great characters and interesting insights into investigating cold cases. I can't wait to read the next book!"
—Reader review for Girl One: Murder

"Very good book… You will feel like you are right there looking for the kidnapper! I know I will be reading more in this series!"
—Reader review for Girl One: Murder

"This is a very well written book and holds your interest from page 1… Definitely looking forward to reading the next one in the series, and hopefully others as well!"
—Reader review for Girl One: Murder

"Wow, I cannot wait for the next in this series. Starts with a bang and just keeps going."
—Reader review for Girl One: Murder

"Well written book with a great plot, one that will keep you up at night. A page turner!"
—Reader review for Girl One: Murder

"A great suspense that keeps you reading… can't wait for the next in this series!"
—Reader review for Found You

"Sooo soo good! There are a few unforeseen twists… I binge read this like I binge watch Netflix. It just sucks you in."
—Reader review for Found You

Molly Black

Bestselling author Molly Black is author of the MAYA GRAY FBI suspense thriller series, comprising eleven books; of the RYLIE WOLF FBI suspense thriller series, comprising six books; of the TAYLOR SAGE FBI suspense thriller series, comprising eight books; of the KATIE WINTER FBI suspense thriller series, comprising eleven books (and counting); of the RUBY HUNTER FBI suspense thriller series, comprising five books (and counting); of the CAITLIN DARE FBI suspense thriller series, comprising six books (and counting); of the REESE LINK mystery series, comprising six books (and counting); of the CLAIRE KING FBI suspense thriller series, comprising seven books (and counting); of the PIPER WOODS mystery series, comprising eight books (and counting); of the GRACE FORD mystery series, comprising eight books (and counting); of the CASEY BOLT mystery series, comprising seven books (and counting); of the JADE SAVAGE mystery series, comprising seven books (and counting); of the ELISE CLOSE psychological thriller series, comprising five books (and counting); of the TESSA FLINT mystery series, comprising seven books (and counting); and of the CLARA PIKE FBI suspense thriller series, comprising five books (and counting).

An avid reader and lifelong fan of the mystery and thriller genres, Molly loves to hear from you, so please feel free to visit www.mollyblackauthor.com to learn more and stay in touch.

BOOKS BY MOLLY BLACK

ELISE CLOSE SUSPENSE THRILLER
BEHIND HER LIES (Book #1)
BEHIND HER SMILE (Book #2)
BEHIND HER SECRETS (Book #3)
BEHIND HER GATES (Book #4)
BEHIND LOCKED DOORS (Book #5)

CLARA PIKE FBI SUSPENSE THRILLER
REMEMBER THE FEAR (Book #1)
REMEMBER THE DEAD (Book #2)
REMEMBER THE LIES (Book #3)
REMEMBER THE SILENCE (Book #4)
REMEMBER THE PAST (Book #5)

TESSA FLINT MYSTERY SERIES
BARELY SEEN (Book #1)
BARELY HEARD (Book #2)
BARELY FORGOTTEN (Book #3)
BARELY MISSING (Book #4)
BARELY ALIVE (Book #5)
BARELY THERE (Book #6)
BARELY SILENT (Book #7)

JADE SAVAGE MYSTERY SERIES
ALL SHE FEARS (Book #1)
ALL SHE WANTS (Book #2)
ALL SHE REMEMBERS (Book #3)
ALL SHE NEEDS (Book #4)
ALL SHE HIDES (Book #5)
ALL SHE DREADS(Book #6)
ALL SHE LOST (Book #7)

CASEY BOLT MYSTERY SERIES
BROKEN (Book #1)

FLAWED (Book #2)
BLEMISHED (Book #3)
DAMAGED (Book #4)
TWISTED (Book #5)
FRACTURED (Book #6)
TAINTED (Book #7)

GRACE FORD MYSTERY SERIES
NEARLY MINE (Book #1)
NEARLY SAFE (Book #2)
NEARLY FREE (Book #3)
NEARLY GONE (Book #4)
NEARLY HIS (Book #5)
NEARLY LOST (Book #6)
NEARLY DONE (Book #7)
NEARLY NEXT (Book #8)

CLAIRE KING MYSTERY SERIES
ONCE HE SEES (Book #1)
ONCE HE LONGS (Book #2)
ONCE HE TAKES (Book #3)
ONCE HE FEELS (Book #4)
ONCE HE KNOWS (Book #5)

MAYA GRAY MYSTERY SERIES
GIRL ONE: MURDER (Book #1)
GIRL TWO: TAKEN (Book #2)
GIRL THREE: TRAPPED (Book #3)
GIRL FOUR: LURED (Book #4)
GIRL FIVE: BOUND (Book #5)
GIRL SIX: FORSAKEN (Book #6)
GIRL SEVEN: CRAVED (Book #7)
GIRL EIGHT: HUNTED (Book #8)
GIRL NINE: GONE (Book #9)
GIRL TEN: WANTED (Book #10)
GIRL ELEVEN: VANISHED (Book #11)

RYLIE WOLF FBI SUSPENSE THRILLER
FOUND YOU (Book #1)
CAUGHT YOU (Book #2)
SEE YOU (Book #3)

WANT YOU (Book #4)
TAKE YOU (Book #5)
DARE YOU (Book #6)

TAYLOR SAGE FBI SUSPENSE THRILLER
DON'T LOOK (Book #1)
DON'T BREATHE (Book #2)
DON'T RUN (Book #3)
DON'T FLINCH (Book #4)
DON'T REMEMBER (Book #5)
DON'T TELL (Book #6)

KATIE WINTER FBI SUSPENSE THRILLER
SAVE ME (Book #1)
REACH ME (Book #2)
HIDE ME (Book #3)
BELIEVE ME (Book #4)
HELP ME (Book #5)
FORGET ME (Book #6)
HOLD ME (Book #7)
PROTECT ME (Book #8)
REMEMBER ME (Book #9)
CATCH ME (Book #10)
WATCH ME (Book #11)

RUBY HUNTER FBI SUSPENSE THRILLER
IF I RUN (Book #1)
IF I TELL (Book #2)
IF I LIVE (Book #3)
IF I FORGET (Book #4)
IF I RETURN (Book #5)

CAITLIN DARE FBI SUSPENSE THRILLER
COME GET ME (Book #1)
COME FIND ME (Book #2)
COME TAKE ME (Book #3)
COME CATCH ME (Book #4)
COME SAVE ME (Book #5)

REESE LINK MYSTERY
BEYOND REASON (Book #1)

BEYOND REACH (Book #2)
BEYOND REPAIR (Book #3)
BEYOND DOUBT (Book #4)
BEYOND NORMAL (Book #5)

PIPER WOODS FBI SUSPENSE THRILLER
SOMEWHERE SAFE (Book #1)
SOMEWHERE SANE(Book #2)
SOMEWHERE WHOLE (Book #3)
SOMEWHERE FAR (Book #4)
SOMEWHERE WRONG (Book #5)
SOMEWHERE HIDDEN (Book #6)
SOMEWHERE DARK (Book #7)
SOMEWHERE SILENT (Book #8)

Printed in Great Britain
by Amazon

53009976R00091